Ten to Thirty

Scott Shaw

Buddha Rose Publications

First Printing 1990

ISBN: 1-877792-54-3
ISBN-13: 978-1-877792-54-0

Library of Congress Control Number:
2011937532

6 5 4 3 2 1 1 0 9 8 7

Printed in the United States of America

Ten to Thirty

4

...CONTENTS

TEN 7

NINE 23

EIGHT 34

night time-EIGHT 46

SEVEN 52

night time-SEVEN 56

SIX 64

night time-SIX 66

night time-FIVE 95

FOUR 102

THREE 102

night time-THREE 106

night time-TWO 113

ONE 140

night time-ONE 146

THIRTY 149

THIRTY + ONE 157

EPILOGUE 180

6

...TEN

Simplicity, I am seeking simplicity.

Somehow though, I suppose that it has forever been the case, my life has begun to spin. Spin, like, more than ever before. No, I cannot say that... That is just my mind: my mind of the now, lost in the now, in the melodrama of the now; the life of the now: where punctuation, it does not seem to matter.

Create, I want creation...

Here I am, the artist...

But, allow me to deviate here, for a moment... To tell/explain the story.

My main, my new and main L.A., Asian, *glam slam,* babe; who I have spent the better part of the last nine months with; who comes complete with all the characteristics of a woman who is full of all of the things I basically dis—like; choices made I do not approve of, and a past un—suited for a perspective goddess.

Naturally, I wish to leave; run away from her.

But, she is made up of all the complete things that seem to take hold and make up all the relationships I enter into in this city. My city; L.A.

Anyway...

As the story goes, we were cruising down Wilshire B.L.V.D. on the day last, en route to having a little breakfast. Breakfast my style, my time, 1:00 PM-ish. She had this little art piece to deliver. For you see she is a graphic artist of sorts, not FA, (Fine Art), but CA, (Commercial Art). A graduate of Art Center, etc...

Anyway, she does these kinds of cartoony pieces that appear in magazines and so on. The night before she had asked me what a French flag looked like. I told her and she placed it in her art piece; for it was a piece for an Asian magazine about Asian art in Paris. She, however, did the flag in the proper order: blue, white, red; left to right. But, she put the flagpole on the wrong side; making it: red, white, and blue. Anyway... Maybe no one will notice.

The point being here is that, I told her, *"Let me go up there with you and meet the head honcho."* In this case being woman. *"I will tell her to get rid of you and hire a real artist. Someone one who breathes art in everything they do, like me."* Actually, I do not even pretend to want a bullshit job like that. As that in not FA by any stretch of the imagination. But, I said it anyway...

Creativity has alluded me a bit over the past several... Well, for long time.

I am a procrastinator, and by definition they are people who expect things to get done all in a moment; when, in fact, they/things take time. But, still and all, accomplishment has not been my better feature of the double feature in this life.

Anyway... Yesterday, there was an e.q. (earthquake), in L.A. It has now been pushing eleven months since the last semi big one. I wrote about it.

There I was L.A., the beach, alone; no one called; again! Not the little West H'wood *glam slam* babe, who I refuse to live with. She has told too many lies. You know what I mean... And, as mentioned previously, a past that would make any mainline Chinese walk away. But, this is L.A. and the Asian babe(s), especially the rich ones, that come here and get their culture(s) all fucked up and generally do end up being former sluts, looking for a man to give them back all that they have lost, fucked up, and thrown away. But, that is a different story...

Now, it could be my space; my apartment, (a bit too small), or my financial condition; deeper than ever in the toilet, or most probably my psychological justification of issues: the why to's they why not's; the let's run outside and spent money: buy something, do something, anything with no purpose at all except the not staying within the walls of a home, (overlooking the ocean, of course). Like yesterday... Post the e.q., (feels like many moons ago but it was just yesterday), a telephone call... She, my main and current L.A. babe, via Taiwan, upset that I had/have so many babes awaiting my return to Asia; a reason to shut down the creative motion, the creative flow... I heard it. I felt. And, in a world where any reason will do; outside, to breakfast, we went. As stated, instead of creativity being created...

You see, it is the dilemma of all bohemians, for there is two sides of the issue and the perplexity: one, stay inside and create;

two, there must be the inspiration to do it/the creativity.

Now Asia...

Seems like as good as time as any to evaluate this/that situation. Let's detail it here; three days past Saturday; today being Tuesday... In any case, this sweet young thing of a Singapore Airline Stewardess who I meet, I guess two plus months back en route from Jakarta to Singapore; there she stood in all her tall Chinese S'pore, (Singapore), blood and beauty. My form... I guess I looked fine to her, as well. Her eyes they could not be removed from me.

Now, being the only person sitting up there in the First Class Cabin, she planted herself next to me and we talked throughout the flight. I was actually on my way to Kuala Lumpur (K.L.) but she extended warm invites to return to S'pore. Things got a little crazy up in K.L., (with love and lust and things in general), and then Bangkok... So, as such and because of, money got a little low, so I eventually headed back to L.A. via TKO, (Tokyo).

I got a postcard from Dubai from her; she was still interested. Then/now, two weeks ago; 29 August, we were to meet in Tokyo and spent some of her vacation together.

Let me tell you, TKO is where I want to be. The spiritual signs, the guidance of my *Spirit Helper,* and everything but my bank account, pointed to my going. I even made reservation two times. But... So, as it goes...

I could have pushed it, the resources, that is; but my energy psychically stolen by my new and current main L.A. babe... As such, I shut down, when I should not have. *No-Go.* I didn't show.

In fact, over the last couple of weeks, when I could have been enjoying the illusion of indulgence in TKO, I instead foolishly spent the same amount of cash that it would have cost to go to TKO on a new bike for her, my main and local L.A. babe, and two for me. I am a fool!

But anyway, she called my telephone answering machine on Saturday. She, the S'pore babe. I was at my pal, Saturday Jim's house. I returned her telephone call. I had to hedge the storyline a bit and give her the not—so—cool lie of, *"Oh, I never received your letter, telling me when you would be there..."*

Born in lies, can never be brought to the truth. Sadly so... But then, I question where can anything lead anyway???

So, she still wants me to come to S'pore and be with her.

My *Scream for the Dream* continues...

I had thought that she and that TKO trip may be my last chance in the *screaming for the dream* endeavor. But, it/my life has proven to not be totally shut down. Not yet, not anyway.

I am still dreaming...

Yesterday, a couple of letters, direct from the far reaches of Asia, arrived in my post office box: P.O. BOX 670. One from this little, more than sweet, young thing. I took a bicycle ride with her in Guangzhou. That was more than a year ago. She still remembers me. She still wants me. I was supposed to show up in Guangzhou last November, 1987. She told me that she was saving her first kiss for her first and only man, who she wanted to be me. Yeah right! But, the thought and the possibility of virgin flesh, (something I have not had for a day or three), is more or less alluring. She still wants me to come and spend my birthday with her.

Letter *numero dos*, from Kumiko san. Kumiko san, my semi sweet TKO babe who is a wanta—be dancer who I met returning from Tokyo's NRT last time around. Actually, I first saw her mount the bus and ride it with me to the international airport from the city. Then, as if some cosmic interception was in place, we rode the moving sidewalks together. I asked her, in Japanese, if she spoke English. She did a little. I did a little, as well... She was off to N.Y. for five days. She had a friend dancing in a Broadway show. She was heading to see said performance. I was L.A. bound.

So, further confirmation... I'm still screaming for the dream.

Continually, I am in the paradox of here/there: Asia/America. There I find. There I live what I want to live. Here is my home. My computer on which I now type. And, though L.A. is semi-cool at times, I live in such artistic frustration here; needing to run out—outside, all the time. Often looking but generally not finding. There, it all comes to me.

My current main L.A. babe, via Taiwan, tells me it is all because I am White, long blond hair, earrings, etc... Because I dress in cool, high fashion; I stand out. And, due to my standing out, the babes dig me. Thus, my ego is stroked, getting what I want etcetera—a~mundo.

No doubt, (dude)...

Any person with any ability at introflection could explain that one to themselves. She/her, my main L.A. babe, is a physical person though. Physical mind/physical desires. In addition to being a CA, she wants to be an FD, (Fashion Designer), as well. In association with Art Center, she has another/secondary high-priced degree from the Fashion Institute; paid for, of course, by her money-ed parents. As such, and because of, she is going to borrow the mega bucks from her best friend's mother to set up her show/her shop/her fashion line...

To sway from the actually point here, (just a bit), that is way no-go in my book; friends and business do not mix, and friend's mother's money and friendship does not mix at all; not even a little bit. But, it is her business—her borrowing; not mine.

Let me paraphrase here a bit further...

Now, I am referring to her, here in this text, as my main and current L.A. babe. Whatever... In actuality, I am in full bail mode from her. The reasons are simple. She likes to lie.

Well, let me explain that a bit better... Though she no longer really does anything detrimental to our relationship; the relationship that never really existed, at least in my mind... Though at times, one, (i.e, me), gets the feeling of trapped up; caught up.

But, that is for another story...

As for her, she doesn't tell her whole stories—which, in my mind, equals lies.

A perfect match for me, right? At least some would say that to be the case in the babe *departemento*. Me, I say, *"No!"*

On top of that, or to better describe it; eight months into our knowing each other session, she drops the bomb on me that she has the *Big H,* (Herpes). Now, I think that is pretty fucked up, someone not telling me that they have something like that until so far into our something. (Thank god, I never got it from her).

It was her belief, so she told me, that I would leave her when I found out. So, she wanted to get me so involved that I could not leave her. If I loved her more, I suppose that would not matter, the *Big H,* but holding the semi—lack of love that I do it is, *"Zie Gin,"* in Chinese or, *"Bye bye,"* baby. Especially knowing the source of the disease; this low-life, no account, French Gypsy mutha fucker, that she used to crib with.

Now, I mean Gypsy are low as it is. So low, in fact, he certainly does not deserve a placement in literature. And, this is my story, not his. *My countdown to thirty.* So, end of that sub-story...

As far as my bailing this babe goes, she does not give up easy. She does not leave me alone. Nor does she take, *"No,"* for an answer.

But anyway...

So, my attachment to her and my distaste for the staying inside or the doing things alone syndrome... And/plus with only the DM, (Dead Meat), babe(s) on the page of local telephone directory, and nothing new yet... Well, fuck... She keeps me going/coming back. Back, to her in her physical perception and/or of life.

But this part, this story, this section is of Asia. I suppose, however, that she, my main and current L.A. babe, is intimately linked with Asia; as she hails originally from Taiwan. And, as such, my desires on the physical side of the picture; at least for her, is all wrapped up in Asia.

And/or, in fact, she is, physically, all I ever wanted. All I ever wanted back then... Pure beauty/pure style. Back then, when I believed in forever relationships/forever love. Yeah, she could have been everything; if everything didn't include her past, and all her lies...

Stated previously, there is more to Asia for me than the physical side. Since I read a book on yoga at six, since I found the *Tao Te Ching* at eleven, since I became a yogi at thirteen, a martial arts instructor at fourteen, so on and so forth...

*   *   *

If I can enter a somewhat journal type of entry here... For that is what life and writing is all-about, anyway... The exit-able main and current L.A. babe, who I am trying to dump, calls me at about this point. Right here/right now, as I write.

Though I have asked her time-and-time again not to telephone me. No, not anymore. But it, the conversation, it was one of the basic go nowhere, upset the both of us convos. Typical, how typical...

Anyway, I ask her not to call again and hang up on her. Then, she calls again and gets upset at what I have to say, while in the process making me upset, and draining my creative energy. So, my life does go on... Hun? And, you wonder why my creativity gets intersected and intercepted.

*   *   *

But, back to the story line...

Actually, if I wish to tell the story, the telephone rang again at this/that point there and another telephone marathon ensued. Going nowhere, saying what has already been said so many items before.

Perhaps, as is the case of my life, a desired distraction/a wanted indulgence where I do not have to view the pagan faces of the reality of my life...

But now, back to the storyline...

It is a bit cool today at the beach. I have just noticed the chill come over me. Usually, September is a fairly warm month. In the city, I am sure that it is still warm; at least warmer. But, this cool is a welcomed relief and it is the reason I choose to live here on the beach.

In fact, I believe that I must go and put on a pair of socks and an over-shirt. (One of those Neil Young looking, too large hippie flannel shirts, that I still have in my possession from way back when... Back, when Saturday Jim and I used to drive up to Canada in the winter and there was a need for a little level of extra warming).

Well, got the shirt on, the socks on, had some apple juice and a banana, and now here I am again.

One pointedness, being the means of accomplishing anything. It is a shame I do not have it.

Asia to me has always held my dreams, desires, illusions, what have you; be they: spiritual, mystical, physical, or otherwise... And, if I had a dollar, I would definitely head over in that direction at this point. There again being the paradox; the creativity of/at home or living the illusion of Asia.

The financial side of life seems to bind so many of us. That is to say, with it, (money), you live it, (life); without it you have zero/you live zero.

Now, spending money, I do it oh so well. Most good psychoanalysts would say it is no doubt due to psychological compensations. No doubt, dude... I know that too. I've lived a lot of the fucked up—fucked up life that is.

But, the spending of, and the purchasing, always seem so logical to me at the time. The only problem being is since about 1984 I have had very little money to call my own.

This, of course, is in no small part due to the fact that I have indulged far too long into artist/mystic passions and have lost all thought to ever being under the hand of guidance of some pseudo—intellectual, stiff asshole, who thinks they are better than me, just because I am an employee. Fuck that! Better to die on your feet than to live on your knees.

It is funny in life; have you ever gotten somewhere and turned around and looked and said to yourself this is not where I had planned to end up at all?

I asked Saturday Jim that question, last Saturday. He answered he thought he would always be a truck driver and now instead he was a carpenter. That was not quite what I meant... He didn't get the question. I didn't pursue the answer.

Me, I always assumed that something would have taken off in my life, and for me, by this point in time. But, it has not.

In some ways, I sit hope and believe that thirty will be it—that it will get better. For all the financial bullshit of the world closes in tight and it causes more pains than it is worth. No fair... Especially to a mystic and an artist like myself.

The main L.A. babe, the one on the previously described phone session(s), today stated, that I should not be so hard on myself for I have accomplished a lot for my age. But, not enough, I think. (My and the world's fault). And certainly, not what I had set out to accomplish.

But, life it is not over yet. And, as R. Buckminster Fuller at thirty found, the voice of God telling him to *just do what he liked*. I hope I too can make such a contribution and a make a living at it, as he has done.

It is like the *take it to the limit* sort of attitude that I have. Few possess it. I have and continue to do so. My life as the representative fact. Most do not, i.e., the S'pore, previously mentioned, babe, *"Why don't you quit and come to visit me in L.A.,"* I asked. *"I can't do that."* Or the TKO NRT flight to NY chick, Kumiko san. *"Why don't you come to L.A. instead, of or at least stop by on your, Stand-by ticket, way back." "I can't."*

You see, most people do not know how to step over the limit/over the line. Even my referred to current L.A. squeeze, who can't seem to develop the ability to take me to dinner because the clothing design business, which she is proposing to do, has not hit the streets as yet, the magazines she has illustrated for have not paid, and her bank account is low. She claims she doesn't want to owe the credit card companies money. She is currently somewhere in the few hundred-dollar rage.

To me, this is all bullshit. For I, daily, take her out to expensive dinner(s), my plastic is up into the ozone range of debts, but I still keep dancing, wishing, hoping that a moment of this madness will equal its weight in the gold of creativity.

So... And... All the babes, I see that they will not take the final step into the abyss for me. Thus, I can only give that partial percentage of myself. And, tomorrow; well, it never knows...

Money, babes, creativity, mysticism... You can see how it all does spin.

*   *   *

my mind goes to a vision

Burma
three years ago
almost three years
not quite yet
almost
a long time ago

the golden mountain
it rose softly above Mandalay
the temperature painted my soul
day time
lost
life long
lost
seeking anything
anything at all
that could answer my question(s)

there was a lady there
one, well maybe two or three
and when nothing equals anything
no answers lost
none were gained
a distant kiss
it caress the sunset
lost days
to lost nights
I did not remain there
long enough

I relieved a letter from her once
once almost
a long time ago

visions lost
vision gained

memories
which mean nothing at all

the colors
the light
the feeling
still young and naive
the lost
not yet knowing
they are lost
I realized it
a bit latter on

so, I would go back
no reason
just no reason at all
another chance
in the dance
Mata Burma
and my soul

*   *   *

1:47 PM, I so rarely ever write in the day. This morning, such as my mornings are, I got up and painted these pages. For what reason? The dream? The lie? Certainly, I do not know. Anyway, it is pushing up on the two o'clock hour. Think I will go and have me a food session over at this little Manhattan Beach place I hit, *The Kettle,* and see what consciousness, life, and the other realms of reality have to offer me.

A lot of people go there, the restaurant that is, few are tuned onto the insight or enlightenment the place has to offer. I guess that is like the stepping over the line; the taking it to the limit. Few ever choose to experience it; few ever know it; that is what makes the few of us; who do know it, different. Different and alone...

And, this day's text, turned out totally different than I had thought it would. Perhaps that is what makes art, art? Whatever happens is the art...

NINE

Scenes...

They always seem the hardest to describe. Like the feeling(s); the vision I had of Burma, day last.

Day last, I almost want to laugh. It is a funny feeling for I am just remembering what I heard on the radio news two days ago; God, that feels like forever ago. But, anyway...

Some NASA scientists, who was a fundamentalist Christian, had done this life-long study and determined that yesterday/day last was going to be the day that the heavens opened up and God pulled all the faith-full up and the rest of us down here were to then endure all of the problem(s) of *The Revelation*. Well, maybe I was just not one of the ones who got pulled up. But...

I remember back when I was a young buck, I had this friend; elementary school, sixth grade. He was an L.A. transplant from Louisiana. His mother was a Jehovah Witness. Once in a while I would go to their ceremonies. I remember them proclaiming that the world was going to end in, what was it, 1974; something like that... And, how this little young dude of a ten or eleven year old, that I was, calculated; *would I have a chance to drive a car—would I be sixteen yet?* Etcetera...

The dude, Steve, was his name, ended up in the joint. Drugs, and proud of the rapes that he had committed. Uncool; very uncool... Ego trippin' about beating up his grandmother. Life... Hun?

But, the scene(s), they are always so hard to describe. I realized that as I looked out my window and onto my patio yesterday.

Scenes, like in Burma.

Scene, like at the hotel I stay at in Bangkok, (B'kok), overlooking the Chao Praya.

I mean, you can see these things in your mind, and I suppose that you can attach words to them; the color(s), if you are not color blind, the movement(s), if you are not blind, and the general picture. Those are all abstract images though. They are not what really is. They are not the actual scene.

I mean, I guess they say some writers, some poets, are very versed at descriptions; making them so artist and so on; but still, that is all that they are; the description of the scene, not the scene(s) themselves.

Living, it is one thing; reading about it is something totally different. The second seems so invalid, so contrived.

OK, OK, history and all you can learn, and it is good that things are documented. It is even good that feelings are documented. I do it all the time. But still, experience outweighs all of that.

Anyway...

My scene outside, that got me going on-and-on about all of this; I don't know... There is just something special about it; if to no one else but me.

I live in this little apartment, with a kinda pull plastic curtain to separate the bedroom area from the main living room. I have been thinking of pulling it out and down. Most of the others who inhabit this building do not even have it up; choosing instead a large single type space to dwell within. Me, I prefer the definition.

I was thinking of installing bookshelves to define/divide the area(s). This method would take my books from their present placement, inhabiting and taking up one entire wall, and making them, and/or it, more functional as a room divider. I don't know... Money it is more than kinda tight right now and I guess in some ways I would prefer to move to large quarters, but...

Anyway, the scene outside... You see, I live on the lower floor; which is actually maybe twenty feet above the beach. Hermosa Beach. I actually live in Redondo though—the city dividing line and all.

On the first floor, the patios are all bigger than the balconies above; way bigger... So, I have a large space outside. In the Fall, Winter, and Spring, I generally paint out there. That is to say when there are not so many people chilling down on the summertime beaches I paint.

But outside, I look, and to my left is the ocean, to my right is *The Strand;* complete with its houses. The Hermosa Beach Pier borders my vision to the North. The Santa Monica Mountains rise to the sky, North of and above that.

How can I say it? With the visual wall just outside my patio and all the picturesque boarders; the sand, it is like a painting. The people are its movements. Like an artist

attempting to paint perfect perspective; a
rectangle going northward. It is done.

* * *

boarders
and waves
people and movement
in the North dwell the sane

the sane and the alive
the fixed and the working
money
it is made up there

to my right
to the East
live the people
        the streets
        the crime
        the lost and the living

houses boarder it here
one million dollars
flowing to shacks
not worth anything at all

here I stand
South
the South
my southern reaches
below me
I do not care
I cannot see there
I do not care there
behind me

is behind me
that
(I point)
is the way I go

      when will I start thinking
      of the future
      when the past stops
      holding me back

to my left
is the ocean
the ultimate frame
West
onto Asia
Asia where I dwell
Asia where I long to be
Asia is everything
      the illusion
      the dream

      I have screamed for it

Asia
the mysticism

out there
over there
to my left

to the left holds mysticism
to the right
holds the night
I am torn between the two

      *   *   *

With all the noisy neighbors, the beach sweeper(s) on the summer mornings; 6:00 AM—I always was a light sleeper—and the space too small for me to be as creative as I like/as I prefer. But, there is something about this place that I do love. The scene, yes the scene.

The scene, like in B'kok; my hotel room(s) overlooking the Chao Praya. The movement(s) on the river; the clouds that paint their abstraction in the Thailand skies—the dance, the nights. I love B'kok. B'kok out of a hotel window; the scene, the growing population, the growing prosperity, the growing poverty, the river, (muddy), the river vegetation floating down, (green), the river, the boats, small, going up and down the Chao Praya, the barges, big. At night there was les noise from their horns that sounded the movements that they made. Movement, always movement; forever movement. The river, the Chao Praya, B'kok, movement...

The mornings when I would sit there, late mornings, early afternoon, with *Do Not Disturb* placed upon my door. A love, such as love is, in my arms, in my bed. I remember her golden skin, verging on brown; black hair— black and long like the night. The nights when you can sleep after you've made love for hours and hours.

Curly, long hair. She had a perm. Her breasts were small. Her lies were big. Her beaver tight and young. Younger than it should have been. She had a child somewhere. A child, I never saw.

Black; her pubic hairs were black. They painted a picture at the base of her crotch; like a downward facing triangle, cut short, stopped tight in a flat ridge.

I remember her the most. The most, thus far, that is... Her, my first Thailand love, my first B'kok chance.

We would sit there, her and I, order late morning/early afternoon *Room Service Coffee.* We would awake very late in the day.

The window, to our side. The river, down below us. We would speak in Thai. We would speak in English. Mostly, I listened to her lies.

Lies, they seem so truthful, when you want to believe.

Yes, back then... Yes, back there... I did believe in forever. Yes, I thought that there was a chance of the love that never dies. I guess that was a long-long-long time ago; if not in years, in age, in cynicism.

Two years. Yes, I was with her, inside her body, two years ago. Three years. Yes, that is when we met and encountered our first touch, our first embrace. She cried, after we first kissed. *"I've never been so in love. I never thought I could ever have a man like you."* So, she spoke. I believed her tears. What a fool.

Thailand, what was it now? Going on three months ago. That was when I was there last. I saw her then too. Well actually, I saw her car; this bad little supped-up, tail finned, VW, with an exposed engine and flames running down its side. Hard to miss! I saw it cruising near *The Pat Pong.* The only ride I ever saw like it in B'kok. Her ride; a ride that looked like that...

Maybe she heard I was back in town and she was lookin' for me. Maybe? I don't know?

Once, a long time ago. Two year(s) ago. We cruised that bad pup up into Northern Thailand; Chaing Rai, via Chaing Mai. Up, there and abouts. Fuck... I won't go into it here. That was a different adventure. A different time/a different mind.

I saw her car though. Three months back... Back, when I was back in B'kok; three months ago. I looked in it. I saw a shadow of her for only a second. She was driving. It was night. Maybe she saw me too. I do not know.

It doesn't matter, however. It was all a long time ago. Her lies, our love; my lies, too.

Too much *pong kow* one night. For those of you who don't know—*pong kow;* powder white; junk, heroin. Her lies they came out. I slapped her when I found out. She deserved it.

The joke, as it always is, was on me. I threw her out of my hotel room. Walked her to the front door of said hotel so I knew she would be *gone-daddy-gone.* I was pissed. I threw her keys out the front door of the hotel onto the ground. She couldn't find them. I, like fucking fool, I helped her look.

Outside/out in front of the hotel/my hotel; late night, out the front door we go... Some dude insults her in Thai. I go up to him. I planned to kick his ass. I needed to kick somebody's ass. He bailed in a hurry when he saw me coming. I report him to the local hotel—police—man. *"This is my wife..."*

What a fucking fool I was.

A scene, a long time ago...

Maybe I get liars, because I lie? Lie for who I am not, what I am not, and who I want to be—who I should be. The world is full of liars.

It is hard to explain to someone that you are zero in a zero world when you are wearing *Rolexe(s), Cartier(s)*, and very expensive clothing—trying to explain to them that you have to leave Thailand; that you don't have enough money to keep up the lifestyle, keep paying the insane cost of living in Five Star Hotel(s) and partying hard on the hard side of the hard road.

Psychological catastrophe in the making...

But, that was that scene; that scene a long time ago.

B'kok, Thailand, oh how I wish to return. With time to kill and money to spill.

I try to visualize the bucks incoming. I try hard to pinpoint the vision I need to visualize.

Viva Las Vegas, my mother wants to meet me her there on the twenty-third. The twenty-third (23), my birthday; nine days away...

Thirty and climbing. I hope, I pray for the money, for the passage, out of credit card/plastic passion debt and the money for the road back to Asia. I think to go to *Viva Las Vega,* I think to go; though I don't want to go. I think to go to and win money. I think/I wish/I dream. Maybe; well maybe...

I will visualize it.

That is then though; nine days, and a five-hour drive latter...

Dutch treat. This is now.

Now, back to, my main, via Taiwan, and current L.A. babe in the present tense. Typical... Yesterday she said she was going to do one thing, then, she made plans for another route, but ended up doing a third. Her first, a path into the Garment District; her friend's mommy's money and all. I have already told that foundational story, however... But, she made plans; trying to get her fashion line launched.

She called me. So, it was traded back and forth; me, seeking a way out said, *"Go! Go for the rendezvous. Go to the Garment District!"* Because I said that—said what she never expected me to say; she decided she would cancel to hang with me.

Actually, I can give her nothing, for I want to give her nothing. I take her out to expensive dinners as I do, expensive gifts as I do, but my heart is not here/not there; not with her. Had there not been all the lies, had there been a way in of a way out, then maybe... But, the big H, and her past following too close on her shirttails; I just can't...

We have this dance going on though; I do not believe that she can see it. The dance: *Destroy each other's lives; as much as possible, to get back at the other one, for something neither one of us ever did.*

That's the name of the game. It is a weird game... Destructive; very destructive.

Actually/personally, I would prefer to simply check out. She won't let it happen though. A call 8:45 AM this morning, to tell me of a bad dream she had of me with another babe in B'kok. *"I wish…"* I told her. Then the drag myself out of bed call 1O:45-ish and the ensuing convo. of life, reality, power tripping and the etcetera.

So, post the cancellation, she planned to go to library, en route and on the way to me, to look up functioning garment manufactures; places where she could get her sewing sewn. Whatever….

Me, I watched a bit of a movie about those who do not succeed on the T.V. Hit a bit too close to home. I turned it off And, then/now/here I sat down at these morning typing keys. Unusual for me, writing in the AM; as stated before…

So there we are and here I am; up to date, non-too late. Awaiting the arrival of a wasted day, with a wasted woman. She is supposed to be here soon.

My life; lived for the literature.

    art and literature
    and all the other
    dreams of a fool

...Eight

the sound I hear
I have heard it before

scream it
once more for me

the feeling
I have felt it

dance it
on my soul
one more time

love
it is for the fool

attachment
for the weak

lust
for the simple minded

give them all to me
one more time

in a distant night
with a distant night stranger
in a place where
she already knows my name

she knows my name
they know my name
call me foolish

call my nothing
nothing to nothing
in a world with no end
a life of too short/too long a time
call me a dreamer
dreams that it might be a different way
call me anything
but what I am
a liar
a seeker of illusion
going from this to that
that to the next
promising everything
when I can give nothing
but then/than
they never gave that much to me

night soars in all its suchness
it cries to me as I sleep
a known touch
a longing touch
longing to know
longing to be left alone
point of view
always setting the rules
and did you know that I loved you
or at least my heart used to fill
with that feeling
now, I am too old
too cynical
too set in my ways
it is all like the world of spirituality
peak experience(s)

life tied up
is life tied down

youth
it was another time

and kisses they hold me
and kisses they lie to me
they turn my world
up-side-down
and the hate in the world
the problems of a life that never was
and what can I do
what do I do
to turn back
the hands of time

turn them back
shut them down
erase all the bad I have ever seen
replace it with only the good
than perhaps
it would be different
perhaps
I do not know
but love and kisses
all of their lies
all of the nights chasing
all of the pain
if only I could erase it

I long for a younger time
a different time
a more innocent time
when pain and control
were not the norm
and there were not so many people
all like rats
that eat themselves

eating each other
seeing who
will be king

I am not
a man of the eighties

*   *   *

I woke up with her next to my side. The main bail—ski L.A. babe. I almost feel like a wimp not having a whole lot more local babes on the line to write about. Asia, now there—there are a few. Here though...

I was awoken way too early, 7:30 AM said the hands on the digital clock. Music alarm and the sounds; a babe who has to go and hit the office.

Now she is in there/over there—going to the office. Me, for you see, I naturally rolled over and went, AOK, back to sleep for a while. It is still early as I write; way too early by my standards: 10:22 AM. I have been trying to keep my way-late night hours, not quite so late night—to bed at two or three instead of four, five, six. There-go, and in that way, I can get some of the daytime things of light done. As often time(s), I chill right-on through the day waking up a bit too late.

My friend, Saturday Jim, always tells me I am missing the best part of the day; the early morning. You see he gets up 4:30 AM-ish en route to the construction site. I tell him, *"Yeah I know, but I see it from the other side of midnight."*

I like the late night; the apparent peace, the silence. Time(s) always seem to change though, and I try to flow with them. Now, in my life; right here, it has meant going to bed a wee bit earlier, for whatever that is worth—as it may all change again tomorrow. My continual jetlag in my own city.

Anyway, the babe, she is off to the office today. To detail the continuing saga, post our convo. Yesterday; she said she was going to hit the B.H. (Beverly Hills) library, then come over. As detailed, coming over was not really in my game plan but I thought if I could complete my morning writing session, *no problema.*

Anyway, long story, short... No show. After a few hours, I called and her roomy. She played me off.

I do not like to be played off. Like, she knew where she fucking was and I did not. Fucking tell me! How fucking stupid!

Pissed me off a bit...

So, the day went on. I had a little B'fast/lunch. I took a bike ride on my bad *Colnago Equilateral* down *The Strand.* I rarely ride *The Strand* in the daytime. I prefer the night, with no people; none of the bullshit competition of the upper-echelon bike riders, so on and so forth.

It was about five o'clock-ish, as I cruised on the cruising on, via my bike ride. It was just as I was thinking about my riding sunglasses and the fact that were perhaps a bit passé due to the fact that the company has now released a newer, bit small, bit more streamline, aerodynamic pair. Anyway, just then/just as I was thinking that this babe passes by me wearing the exact same shades as me, in the opposite direction. Then, back the other way, we pass again—opposite directions and all...

Mostly, what I am seeing here/there was/is this babe all smiles at me. As such, a little interest arose... I will have to go for another ride today; same time-ish...

In any case, I was showering; post the ride and the telephone rings, *"Hello." "Don't hang up."* I guess she, the main via Taipei, L.A. babe has gotten used to my usual response to her and her telephone calls; especially when she has pissed me off.

She goes into the story. I go into the power trip.

Well, it's called power-tripping baby but that's alright with me.

A little ditty, take off on, *The King,* that I came up with forever ago. I was maybe fifteen years old. Anyway...

Basically, it went back and forth, through three telephone calls, or so. I, hanging up, naturally...

It went on that she loved me so much and that she was trying to do what would make me happy. Thus, she had not gone for the Garment Distract or to the library; in order to set up the company with her friend's mommy's money, and all. But/instead she had called around for a freelance job; got one and went for it, due to all the bills which she has to pay.

"You don't love me, You don't really care about me, do you?"

So, the question rang in my ears over the telephone lines.

How do you tell a person that, in fact, you do love them as much as is possible and though you know the relationship can't go anywhere, you still have feelings for them. Thus, you are still together, still trying to leave, while your own life is coming down around you.

I ask this question, for I have; time-and-time again, tried to explain the situation to her and she has not listened; she has not heard me. It must just be due to the fact that she; growing up in the high society/big money of Taipei and later O.C., (Orange County), plus the fact that she/the Chinese don't think about anyone but themselves. All that, (and more), equaling her bloodline/mentality, and mostly her own, self-developed pig headedness...

But, now, as to the main premise being; and the fact that, as previously mentioned, she has handed me some shit upon occasion; early on in our relationship. Based on, who she is/what she has/had been/become.

Allow me to explain; go a bit deeper...

I mean, when you come right down to the fact of the matter; post Taipei, she grew up in the O.C. Then, as all the typical tourist babe(s) do, who move to West H'wood; thinking it is so fucking hip and cool; they walk down a wayward road to *no-wheres-ville-daddy-o*. I mean they all spread their legs for anybody. I know, because a lot of them have spread their legs for me.

In any case, and etcetera, how and or why she thought it was AOK to talk to a few of her old dudes, (who had spread her legs), in order to get a job or for whatever reason, (when I was not around watching), is just not righteous.

You see, I go for totality. Yes or No. This or That. So, it/her action(s), no doubt, pissed me off a bit; once I found out what she had been up to.

Sure, it was no big deal: no sex, no going out, or anything. To a self—actualized, *let's flow with it,* sort of person; it would be *no problema* at all. Sorry, that is not my style.

So basically, she has been doing everything in her power to make up for those incidence(s) for the last eight months of our nine-month relationship. That is except for the two months in which I bailed for Asia; not telling her, just sending her a post card, from LAX.

Scream for the Dream, I did party down. Double Standards, yes. I know. Yes, I know, and I don't care. That is the way it is if you want to be with me.

If I can get a little bit deeper into this subject though... You see, it is the basic case of allowing yourself to be with somebody that you do not really wish to be with. This seems to be the story of my relationship life. A fool, hun? So, everyone pays the price.

She begs to marry me, live with me, be with me forever. She does not even really know who I am.

Like the comment she made last night before we were off to *sleepy—bye—land* about how stupid this one guy was on the radio yesterday, speaking of being spiritual. As I told her, you only say that because you are not spiritual. This is not a value judgment, just an observation.

But, back to the subject at hand: her call/her job/her not telling me...

After the three telephone conversations, and my power tripping, due to the fact I like things neat and clean, pigeonholed, as it goes; i.e., the clear and obvious truth from my babes...

You see, *and perhaps the funny thing about all of this and the reason I was more-or-less forgiving was,* she didn't call me until post her job, due to the fact that they wouldn't let her use the telephone. Why? Because the last time, when she was freelancing there, while I was *Screaming for the Dream,* she kept calling Asia Five Star Hotels trying to track me down. Calling them on their dime.

So anyway... funny, huh?

Yesterday/evening last, she called me, and we spoke from her apartment. Afterwards, (after the call), I took a nap; awoke to a telephone call from the VFA trying to sell me stuff. And then, she was there/here.

There she was, standing at my door, inside my door; pure artistic perfection. Her hair, black; black and long. The front moused up just a bit, making it reflect in the dimming light of the night. Exposed; steel toes, on the black shoes which I had purchased for her. Pants, she wore. And, though I prefer the classic long skirt look, the Persian Midnight Blue of them framed her hips oh so well. Her shirt, rust colored; caressing her white skin/her black hair. There can be no doubt, she certainly is a babe.

Laying in each other's arms. Ah, it is special—special like no one before...

The lights were out, except for the blue light which glows in this little neuvo—high tech aquarium I have sitting over there on the stereo speaker. It was like it always is, the magic.

Our personalities clash, to the max. But, our pillow talk, it is so real.

Pillow Talk, she says that is all I ever do/give to her. But then/there/it is all so real: the feeling, the love, and the magic. Once we are outside of that, the world comes crumbling down upon us.

We played a bit. My hand in her Asian pants. I eventually had to pull them down to take a look at her more that sculpted body. There is a certain perfection in the lines of her form. Even as I write, that feeling of love and perfection takes me over. But, now/here/in this moment as I write, she is outside the realm of pillow talk, at an office; probably speaking to other office men who try to move in on my babe.

If she would go away, they could have her. The problem is, she won't go away. So, they can't have her.

Addiction, in my veins. Like a drug that will not leave you alone. If she were a drug, I am sure she would have the legs to chase the junky.

As I stared at her body, she pulled down my pants and grabbed the areas around my dick so well—like only she has had the ability to do.

We lay there deep in embrace for a time. The only illumination coming in from the ocean lights on *The Strand*. It cut her perfectly, like the shading I have always longed to find in my photographs.

We lay on the bed, her shirt up, my shirt up, her chest touching mine. I got her off with my hand. And then, for a while, a long while, we made love.

There is/was again, all that electricity, for lack of a better word. That feeling that only she has given me. That feeling, upon insertion, of the chill up my spine, of, *this is where I am supposed to be.*

It was dark. It was the night. Her midnight blue pants down around her ankles, held on by her black exposed steel-toed shoes. My dark blue pants pulled down. We lay on a black metal bed, atop a black comforter. Her black hair merging into the absence of light. Dark it was all dark, as the night generally is.

There I was again, the perfection of the pillow talk; the perfection of the prefect joining of the perfect bodies, no way in/no way out.

She was getting me involved; way involved.

But, time for the movies were at hand. It was she who had wanted to go. She, not I. She who needed the distraction from an inclosing life. So, I pulled out, pulled up, *"If we are going to go we had better go,"* I said.

The movies, AOK: popcorn, a hot dog, and a diet coke. They never sell *bonbons* anymore.

Home in my bad little *1964 Porsche 356 SC.* Into the night realms again.

We lay down in bed. *"I have to go and brush my teeth." "No,"* she said and kissed me. We made love. Made love for a very long time.

So that is the story, you may see how I am torn between a woman who I cannot help but love in her perfection and cannot help but hate the rest of the time. What do I do?

Keep your opinions to yourself actually. I really don't want to hear them.

*   *   *

My curtains have remained closed this morning. Hidden from the outside world.

Thursday, this is Thursday. The day I usually go to FM, (Farmers Market), eat a little Belgium Waffle, have a little Cappuccino, and read the new *L.A. Weekly.* But, that it far. Far from where I live. Far from where the ocean meets the sand. Do I feel like going today? I don't know. I guess so... Go: for the illusion/for the chance.

With every dance there is another chance.

...night—time EIGHT

Time.

Do you ever think about time?

If you live as long as I do, you will be as old as I am.

I think the first real feeling of time *closing in on me,* came; what was it, maybe four years ago? I remember it well. I was in my rather larger apartment; the one over in Hermosa Beach; two blocks off of the beach. The kind with the 1960's ugly green shag carpeting and the plaster, (not dry wall), walls. But, that is beside the point.

I remember there was a movie on T.V., Channel Five (5), I think, *Uptown Saturday Night,* with Bill Cosby and Sidney Poitier. I was removing canvas, which I had painted on, from their stretcher bars and rolling them. I was not enjoying the time and I remember it taking so long to do the job; so many canvases. I remember feeling that, *what a waste of time this is!*

Since then, that time, it has seemed to close in even more. All the mundane things should be accomplished by those with their minds less turned towards the arts, towards mysticism. Thus, all things being accomplished by people who are gaining from the experience.

Certainly, I am not trying to say that maids, factory workers, art helpers, and the etcetera, are not equally well intentioned but they/their life has chosen another path.

Path, that is a funny thing, and how we get thrown into it. Do we choose it? Or, do we allow ourselves to be thrown into it?

I remember this taxi driving pair one Summer in Shanghai; a little over a year ago. God, it feels like forever ago... But, the one dude; they were brothers: drove; the other rode shotgun; he did not know how to drive. It was a family taxi. No doubt a large accomplishment in the People's Republic of China in the 1980's. The father drove it in the day, the brothers at night.

I liked him, the shotgun rider. I liked them. Each night, post my date with my Shanghai lady, I would look for them near the *Peace Hotel*. Often times, they would wait for me. Wait, post our dinner, our coffee session, our dance(s) into the long walks, with all eyes upon us, in the scalding hot summer nights of Shanghai. Wait for us to look for them; to take my babe, (of the city), home into the realms of the not so fortunate. Then, drive me to the *Hua Ting Sheraton*; the most elegant hotel of the/in the city at the time.

The crowds they would stand outside. Stand outside and stare.

This bad shotgun rider once asked me what I did. A question I never like to answer. *"An artist,"* is my general response. He too liked art. He too wanted to be an artist. But, his family, his country, his culture, and his taxi did not allow him to do such a thing.

Destiny?

So anyway, we all do what we do. Time it does take its toll and the price(s) are forever too high.

When I turned twenty-seven, the hours, they seemed to begin to shift against me. I had felt by than that I would be somewhere, someplace else. I was not.

Now, I try to stop the spinning, try to experience the experience, try to create. Psychological condition, life, destiny, and bad childhood experience(s), they all lead to the functioning, or the dysfunctioning there-of and there-fore.

It/they have created the artist. It/they have formed the mystic. That is, who and what, I am. But, I cannot say; basically due to negative programming and faltering financial conditioning, that I am all that happy with the ramifications of being the above said.

So, I do the laundry with as much clear intent as possible. I clean my apartment with as much consciousness as available. I try to learn from everything. But, I must admit, there are generally things that I would rather be doing with my time than wasting it on the mundane.

Time to kill and money to spill.

That was another time, a time ago...

So now, riding in the car has become a chore; though I try to use the time as consciously as possible: studying foreign languages on tape, studying new musical styles, listening to little-known composers, listening to the Talk Radio, and radio shrinks.

But everything, it all seems to add up to nothing; no matter what you do. It, in the end, means nothing.

So, I do not fool myself that art or mysticism has any better a purpose than anything else. It is all just a state of mind.

And, anything that I can do, can be done, just as well, by someone else.

All the art has been done. All the philosophy spoken, (no answers). And, if Einstein had not done what he had done, someone else would have; that is just the way the world works.

Purpose, it for the believer(s). But, the believers are the fools—fooling themselves, that life means some-thing, when in fact it means no-thing; not a goddamned thing at all.

Negative; no, just realistic.

And the time, it comes down on you. What can you do? Sometimes you feel good, sometimes you feel bad. Better to feel good than bad, yes?

Point of view and who knows what it will all lead to. One thing leads to another.

It, in fact, amazes me how one thing... Something you may never have expected, leads you to something new, different, even great. Like being the only two people left in the Shanghai airport without a taxi; without a ride. Her, the most beautiful woman in Shanghai, and me, a jet-set bohemian.

So, I try to slow the spinning down; dream: live the dreams. But, more-and-more, as time has passed, I seek, need to hold on to, need to see immediate results, or I feel, time is wasted.

*   *   *

time wasted
like the art
no one sees

the art
that no one cares to see

like the notes
played a million times
by a lonely musician
for no one's ears
but his own

time wasted
like the loves
that were
the loves
that never were

not really
leaving themselves open
to the only road possible
to make them something
recorded
as literature
maybe someday/somewhere
in some greater place
it will all have accumulated
and meant something more

*   *   *

My babe, you know the one, tall,
Chinese, beautiful; tonight, she wore a Santa
Cruz style hippie design, dress set to the
movies. Now, she lay fully nude. What a
beautiful body. Cloaked in the shadows of the
night.

She lay sleeping, asleep in my bed. This is the late night, my night, and she has a job to be at tomorrow: 7:30 in the AM.

She came over, we touched, we held, we lay down within each other's arms. Out to out; we return. She was tired.

Four years younger; she looks older than I. (I guess it is due to all those years of smoking). We made love. Very special love. We spoke. We always speak. We have a very verbal relationship. She went to sleep; I went to write. This is some of the product.

Zero in a Zero world.

...SEVEN

dead time
no time
killing time
in a wasted time afternoon

turn the T.V. on
Transformers
cartoons
animation
for the 1980's of the 1980's
one of the dudes
even had a pony tail

thirty minutes down
stare outside
I was out there once today
no place to be
nothing to see
I have been there
I have been here
all too many times before

those with a reason
those with a purpose
working nine-to-five

2:57
take me to heaven
if I had anywhere else to be
you know that I would surely go

everything is waiting
it is all for the taking

I flash back to a night—time dream

over a bridge
to a place
the place, I no longer remember where

a place
like any place
a time in no time
living for the poetry
living for the art
living for the mystical
the artist/the mystic
always seems
to be living alone

any other way
any other game
I don't know
how else could it have been played

days with no reason
night living the treason
in love with a babe
who I don't want to love
she is out there
in the real world
as I told a waitress, who knew us, today

"Real world, I have heard of it."
"I think it some place out there."

letter in the P.O. Box
Shanghai, the return address

a year ago

a life-time ago
she tells me
that she has a cat
a black cat
brought home from Xian

she hopes I will love it
for she loves me
she hopes I will love it
for she loves it

love it
when I return for her

love a year ago
love a letter ago
love a year latter
a letter a year latter
love
it seems like forever ago

so dance on the souls
dance with a fire
purification
by any other means

life and dreams
moments and screams
where do I go
what do I do
that proves anything
that makes me anything
that isn't just another lie

*   *   *

Funny, I look around myself here and there is so much to do. I have a new bicycle frame which I had picked up a week ago today; a *Bottecchia,* laying on the floor awaiting assembly. But...

I have handlebars which need to be changed on my *Bianchi, Super Grizzly* ATB. But...

Years of poetry and prose to transcribe. But...

Volumes of aphorisms to collect, organize, and place upon disk; to be placed upon paper, to be collected in a book. But...

In actuality, it is almost amusing, that the very first book I actually wrote was a book of saying; aphorisms, if you will. Back in 75...

Just today, (late 1988), I sent it/them, the stuff up until 1980, in for copyright.

I suppose by whatever means there is creative things being accomplished.

I painted a painting today and my computer floppy disk section of completed works is filling up. But, I have so many books already written, so many more in my mind; and so many more continually coming; i.e., even this one that is quite a task to work on; as the alone of the inside walls close in. I guess that is why people work, out there, in the real world.

Glass walls to the ocean forms the isolation.

...night—time SEVEN

If I wake up before ten o'clock I generally feel fucked for the rest of the day; this being the case of today. In fact, that has been the case of the last two days. Thus, *uck* build-up has occurred.

It used to be if I rose before 8:00 in the AM, then/now it has pushed itself later to 10:00. With two days of rising at 7:30; walking the babe, (you know the one), to the car——the gentlemanly thing to do and all... And then, trying to un—effectively crib back down. I feel like shit.

I have not been sleeping well lately anyway. The FA of napping, (it is a fine art you know), has not even been very restful.

Turbulent(s) in the psychic wind.

The chick, you know the main and central one, she is now asleep. Came over; though I did not really want her. Arrived all prepared and prepped-up for two-birthday parties tomorrow.

One and first; her roomy, Deborah. A relatively nice and certainly fine image of another Chinese-American babe. If I had the chance... But, my current situation is already way too complicated.

Second and two, her *'Ba,'* father, for a little Chinese get together with the family in a restaurant in Monterey Park; $100.00 a plate.

Me, I do not dig parties. Bullshit people saying bullshit things. I am supposed to attended both; purchase all the gift(s); supposedly from her and I.

Her and I. But, my money. Her and I—
yeah right!

I have decided instead to chill, exit stage
left. Tomorrow is Saturday, Saturday Jim's day.
There it is easy: nothing to be, nothing to do,
just myself; the perpetual zero.

She is asleep. No doubt she will awake
early; AGAIN and expect me to wake, as well.
It will assuredly piss me off. So, prediction in
the mind's eye, inconsideration in its wake, and
there are so few bohemians left in this world.

But me, I sit here at these late-night
keys, an *Ice Java* over to my side. *Ice Java,* it
does bring back memories. Memories of Asia.
Memories of flight(s) to Asia. *"What would
you like to drink?" "Ice coffee, please."
"What?"* There are so few bohemians in this
world.

Ice coffee, forty—thousand feet; where
I am, who I am; as the rapture of the trans—
oceanic sound blows the mind of my ears.

*   *   *

listen stranger
listen to who you are
feel it
know it
no-where to be
no-thing to see
but see it all
every-where/every-thing
 kiss me distant traveler
I need to be kissed by you
again

* * *

It has dawned into a new day over here; the words, the pages, the written...

As I am saying nothing. It became the truest statement of art; yes?

I suppose there are story(s) to tell, scene(s) to remember, and situations(s) to describe. But, there purpose escapes me at this moment.

Well one... Maybe just one...

It was B'kok, last time around. Down from my Five Star Hotel into a Minus Two Star World.

This babe; I had met her on the plane; K.L. (Kuala Lumpur) to B'kok. Involved with another dude but needing a Thai interpreter. Malay, Chinese. That's what she was. Kuala Lumpur her street address... She was fine.

We were out. She was shopping. I hate shopping. I love buying. But, I hate shopping.

It began to rain. We checked into an *A&W Root Beer Stand;* no jive/no lie. We sat there and watched the Thai rain come down— attempted purification at a world, a culture, a civilization, that seeks none.

It was so fucking romantic... That is to say, as fucking romantic as it could be, latched in with a babe, (and I do mean a babe), attached to another man, as she was.

Anyway, that was the day before; the before, the actual occurrence. Nothing really jumped. Though I certainly would have been a willing participant if it had.

To make the long story short, at one of our shopping jaunts, I chilled upon this little tailor made suite sales—babe, *"Tomorrow, I will come back tomorrow."* I told her.

I did, and in fact, came back, day next, to buy my first handmade in Thailand suit(s).

Now, I mean the majority of my clothing is Italian made. It/they all range in the realms of the mega bucks. But, I found that there, B'kok, I could design my suits exactly as baggy and as stylish as I liked, for close to *nada* in the *danaro,* or should I say, *"Baht," departamento.*

So, I ordered up a couple. They would be done *manyana.* The babe said she was twenty—one. Actually, I really didn't care. We made dinner plans.

Here I was again, one thing leading to another... Damn if it is not amazing.

But, then the world, the Thai world, and the Goddess of Thailand, all began to close in on me.

Next, a bit later that day, I had met two babes that were seriously into my style of *falong,* (foreigner). Post that, I set up a meet with a more than serious hotel cashier of a babe; closer in proximity to my age and time.

Eight o'clock rolls around. The two babes, previously mentioned, out of nowhere give me the call. I invited them up to my room overlooking the Chao Praya. They were initially a bit shy. Initially, but then... But, that is a different story. You can imagine the happenings; until said happenings are scribed into some other piece of literature.

Then, the previous choice; the young suit-selling babe waiting for me downstairs. She calls... Downstairs, waiting... Me, I wanted to chill her off, head on, and go for the older cashier.

Shaving cream on my face, torn in the middle of panic, 8:00 PM w/ her, 10:00 PM set w/ the other... I had made date(s) with both. Make a choice. You must make a choice!

I want? Do I want? What do I want???

The telephone rings. I had to go and meet her; the younger one—the suit maker one. I slid down around the side way so as the actual one of my choices; the Five Star Employee would not witness the *rendezvous*.

Her, she, Thai. I think of her now; the hotel cashier...

Interesting how I met her.

Side-Story here...

The power had gone out/down in the hotel. I could not use my In-Room Safe. Down I went to store my stuff in the Hotel Lock Up and Safe Deposit Box.

It was dark. I buzzed to be let in; no lights, only candlelight. Warm, no *air-con*. Hot, like only Thailand can be. I looked around myself. I, in the room. The babe in the room. Proper English would have paraphrased that statement in the opposite direction. There was hotel bars between us, but it did not stop the connection—*tear down the walls!*

I do not even remember how it started but I remember asking, *if/was she was married?* Her answer was clear, plan, blatant; like some wild rabid mutt in heat, *"No, nobody loves me." "I will love you,"* I immediately said.

It was all like some seedy 1940's high budget black & white movie. From there the rest is history...

That night though, two date(s) in hand. I though, *'Well I can chill them both; two birds in the hand, being better than my hand not being in any bush.'*

So, no way out, no way in.

I met her, the younger one. I took her to the best restaurant in the hotel, of the Five Star World. She didn't eat a thing. Had never experienced western food.

Money and me... A hundred dollars plus spent on her meal alone; and she didn't touch it. A drunken old *Aussie* walks by, comes up; says, *"You must be from Australia."* *"No, California."*

I don't like Aussies.

She wanted to go to a disco. I took her to the best disco in town. She held my hand; told me she was *really* only nineteen; told me she was a virgin. Wanted to know if I would like to love her. Wanted to know if I would rent a room in this other hotel for the night. The other/mine, to close to her place of employment.

Somehow, I didn't get it. Somehow it slipped right out of my hands. Somehow the bullshit just bleeds through. Somehow, I was saved by the goddess or maybe tossed to the hounds of hell; it all depends how you want to look at it.

Life in Thailand; like a beautiful, dead hard-on, hooker who had asked me to dance a year the previous, and I had drunkenly said,

"No." Her pagan image has haunted me ever since.

She, like her, (the young girl), I foolishly let slip away. Me, I watched the hands on my *Rolex*. I watched the time for the meet with my other woman of preference slip by/slip away. I watch it slip into *never-never-land*.

I took her home; the girl—the young girl in a taxi. An hour, on the outskirts of B'kok, each direction.

Hot, it is always so fucking hot in Thailand.

Since then, she has haunted me too... It seems every time I leave B'kok, there is this fool-hearted reason to fulfill my lost, not yet known, lust and return. There always seem to be that one untouched/unknown; that I should have known that I could've have known, image of promised light in a life of darkness.

Life and the penis of a mystic and a bohemian.

The taxi driver and I had a way good convo. though...

*   *   *

So as seven AM approaches far too fast, as I dwell here on the far side of midnight, I suppose; for lack of anything better to do, I will sip my last gulps of this night—time's melting ice, *Ice Java*, I will kill the last drops of grape from this bottle I drink, and I will go and lay down next to my current addiction, (you know the girl), and dream it was another way; dream I was another time; dream I was somewhere/someway else—with somebody else.

    For whatever dreaming is worth...

...SIX

lamination
illumination
in the night
her watch
glow in the dark
lights the pagan blackness
of my bedroom

faded green
almost green
the most mystical of colors
she lay there
her arm exposed
faint numbers
faint watch hands
I look at her
my attention
is brought to them

black covers
on a black steel bed
her black hair
merges into the night

black on black
no way back
the watch
I bought her
leads me to a poem

thirty seconds
then I will be gone
phone call from Saturday Jim's wife
lO:15 AM
invite to dinner
invite to the night
first time ever
A~O—K
the babe is pissed
typical…
as typical be
breakfast and promises
that I will be there
when I know I will not
she was off
I am off
late as usual
feeling rushed as usual
I guess…
I choose my own path

...night—time SIX

Ever so slightly tilted...

Head Banger videos on the TELa—VISion.

The morning; woken up to the telephone ring: my main, my trying to bail, L.A. babe, via Taiwan, sleeping, (well, at least in the bed), to my tune—amazing, it was 10:15 and she was still in bed...

Saturday Jim's woman, on the love bucket line; invites me to a dinner in my honor; AOK—my upcoming B'day and all...

The chick pissed. What else is new?

But, let me go back, an hour or so before...

I lay sleeping, well semi-sleeping; awoke a few minutes before by her, the babe, crawling over me to hit the head—small bladder, she does this several times a night.

Back in the sack, *"Take your clothes off! Why are you sleeping in clothes. You never sleep in clothing?"* She asks, says, questions... *"Well, when I want yours off, I just take them off."* I exclaim.

For some reason, I just laid out/crashed out with mine on, evening last. Hit the sack jack and that was that.

Me, I like to sleep naked; generally, but especially when there is a babe in tow.

She, my main and current L.A. babe, she has this thing; security and all, about sleeping in underwear, and preferably clothing.

Her uncle, back in Taipei, used to enjoy taking her into the *Play-Room* and finger-popping her—finger-popping when she was way young. Obviously psychological damage incurred. So, I understand...

I'd kick that mutha fucker's ass given the chance. DO NOT MESS WITH CHILDREN!

This morning, she took my clothing off. I have spoiled her, I guess. Spoiled her into the realm(s) of the naked sleep.

Anyway, we were laying there, pre the telephone ring. I was, as I generally do, admiring her oh so fine bod. The love motion was in session.

The scene. Well, fuck the scene! I was into her, way into her; if you catch my meaning?

But, then it flashed... Nine months into her. It had/has never been this way/that way before; nine months and still in-lust. I still liked her body.

Love/infatuation/whatever, (that fucked up feeling), was covering me like the rancid smearing of peanut butter. Idol worship.

The pup was in motion. I was in the mood. Then, the telephone call...

She was none too happy with the fact that I stopped doing what I was doing and answered it. I knew that I knew who it must be...

She was more pissed that I was AOKing a *rendezvous*. She had wanted me to/ had planned for me, to attend her roomy's surprise birthday party; 3:00 PM. Then, head on and over to her daddy's birthday party, seven in the PM in Monterey Park.

The actuality of the situation(s) and the truth being told, I had no desire to go to the either of them; parties not being my scene. Furthermore, she had planned that I was the one to purchase the both of them, (her roomy and her daddy), the presents from, "Us." Some nerve, hun? I think I already mentioned all this...

It was like the night before, her asking me why I never bought her any gifts. Babes, they always talk of what you don't do—not of what you do; i.e. and in example there-of, I mean come on... I just purchased her this mega bucks Italian mountain bike, the week before, and a *Tag Heuer*, the day before that. But, no biggy; right?

So, post our fuck session, (good as it was—as it always is), I had to take her out to breakfast; en route, I had to tell her she was just and still is a *cha—cha,* (what she like to refer to Chinese party girls as). What she used to be... Nightclubs and parties; hollow, and mindless—a perfect creature in the arm(s) of the undeserving.

For a moment sometime, like this morning, I almost forget what she has/had been. Stupid, I know... Stupid, my forgetting...

In any case, as stated, I ended up taking her out to breakfast; promising to show at the daddy's party; saying I would purchase a gift en route.

She had a five-hundred-dollar watch in mind—so she suggested... Yeah right!

In reality, I never intended to do the either. The party(s) or the watch.

Post the breakfast and our farewell(s); me, I went and purchased a new suit for myself, (for my B'day dinner of the oncoming evening), and a pair of mini binoculars.

Let me paraphrase here if I may; if only for just a moment...

Life, desires, visualization, *Spirit Helper(s),* and the etcetera. Binoculars in my mind; a flashing glance that it would be special if they were on sale for, $69.00. Enter the store. On sale, $64.99, plus tax, equaling, $69.00 & something cents.

Life and Projection and somehow when you are focused on the metaphysical it equals the feeling of equaled Perfection.

Perfection, when it all falls into place.

Perfection...

So, post all that, a bit of a mindless rush to Saturday Jim's. A rush, *por nada,* as he had not even gotten home from his Saturday labor. (Sometimes he works on Saturdays). And, the Saturday dentist appointment he had; that I did not know about/was not told about; until I arrived.

In any case, prior to his arrival, I watched a German movie, with his Dutch wife, and played *hide-the-things* with their little girl; (my goddaughter). She's a cutie...

He and I, S.J. and me, we go way back... Ten, fifteen, twenty years. The stories, they are endless.

*   *   *

Saturday Jim and I used to head out on our scoots on Saturdays. Am I being redundant? Saturday Jim and Saturdays? So, I will just say, S.J. and I used to take our motorcycles out for little drives around town on Saturdays. Is that better?

That was, of course, when we were younger and far more foolish—long before we both got our facial structures rearranged by the meeting of face to pavement via our motorcycles—via very-serious, life-altering motorcycle crashes.

This Saturday, the Saturday that I speak of/reminisce about; a Saturday a long time ago... We did what we did with little exception. Little exception, except for the fact that S.J.'s bike was in the shop, having a personality crisis or something, so he was riding shotgun on the back of mine.

Now, we had put in our usual session at the Saturday pizza parlor; *Shakey's* over on Santa Monica, B.L.V.D., in Hollywood; where we consumed our usual large pizza (each) and a pitcher of beer (each). How we used to do that and stay slim is far beyond me??? We also had done our session, a little walk around, at Venice Beach.

We were traveling East—East on Santa Monica B.L.V.D. East, toward the crib of S.J. We were cruising, it was mid—day, one, two, or so, in the afternoon, and my bike; as bad as it be, begin to shut down on us—us: S.J. and I. It was not sputtering and spurting, it was just shuttin' down...

Then, down it went. No electrical.

We, S.J. and I, decided it must be the battery. So, in pursuit of the aforementioned, we went... The bike, in park mode by the side of the road, Santa Monica B.L.V.D., East—over in latter part of Santa Monica verging on the W.L.A.

The Yellow Pages, "Let your finger do the walking," and all, set the course of action for the call of the play of the day. No real motorcycle dealerships around, so we headed for the next best place or thing, or so it seemed to be—a motor scooter shop.

It was a walk... It was Fall. But, it was none to cool, if you know what I mean. We went East. East on S. M. B.L.V.D. East from the latter part of S.M.

See, I used S.M. instead of Santa Monica to not be redundant...

The scooter store was on Westwood B.L.V.D. So, it was a strut. The thought crossed my mind to put in an appearance at a Martial Art Studio on S.M. B.L.V.D. that we walked past, where I knew the owner, (a friend of the man who I ran a studio and taught martial arts for), where maybe we could get a ride. But, the thought was disintegrated by S.J.

Properly so... For, the dude in question, a Korean, would probably have laughed at us and told us to take a hike—which we were doing anyway. So, why bother...

Aside from that thought expedition, and the moment when we stopped in at a local liquor store to pick up a few cold ones for the road—a liquor store where we thought we were going to have to blaze up a bunch of Mexicans, trying to be bad, out-front. But, they weren't very bad. Confronted, they peed their pants. The walk continued...

We hit our mark, made our score, probably an hour or so into the adventure. They obviously didn't have the battery needed—needed for a real motorcycle, but we took the closest thing available. I paid the nice old English guy in plastic format and instead of hoofing it back to our point of origin, we grabbed a passing taxi; battery in hand.

The new battery in, the old battery left by the side of the road: S.M. B.L.V.D., East; we were back on our way.

Our intention to hit big S.J.'s crib; shower and change into suitable attire and hit Westwood for our, then traditional, go see a movie, than hit the bar and impress the crowd with our intoxication abilities. Then, walk out straight and cool, proceeded by falling all over and holding each other up until we got on our scoots and drunkenly drove to a zone of safety; generally, back to S.J.'s aunt's crib, (Aunt L), also in Hollywood, where we were always welcome, and there was always a party going on.

Now, that was our plan... But, plans as you may know, do not always come to be...

We were heading East; East on S.M. B.L.V.D. As we drove—passing us in the opposite direction, came a car: white, Japanese. Inside, low-and-behold, two babes. We: S.J. and I, of course, noticing this because we: S.J. and I, being as all *'Dudes'* be, had this knack of seeking out and scooping in on any babe(s) in the territory.

Now, they cruised on by and flashed the peace sign in our direction. A peace sign? Now come on; *which way to the sixties?*

But, they being *babes*, and we: S.J. and I being *dudes;* naturally I turned the bike around and in their direction we headed.

We proceeded to follow next to them and talk—follow and talk in a wayward, nowhere objective.

"Oh, we like your hair."

They exclaimed.

S.J. and I having long hair; ponytail tied, for the wind/the ride and all.

"Well peace to you too."

The Greatful Dead blasted on the their car's tape machine. Uck, *The Greatful Dead,* S.J. and I agreed.

They, the babes, not *The Greatful Dead,* were alright. One brown haired, the other sandy blond. They were young. We knew it even then. But, we were only twenty-one. So, if they were old enough to drive; a party was in the works…

Now, this little adventure, this little conversation, this little drive proceeded to the realms, round-and-about, of Palms, Culver City, or something. It proceeded until we were invited within the confines of their automobile—destination, a drive onto Malibu.

The invitation in truth came none-to-soon; for, as it turned out, my bike was on a downward trend again. It wasn't just the battery after all. And, in fact, I coolly coasted the bad boy up to the curb; though they, (the newfound babes), never guessed that a thing was wrong.

*   *   *

And, as all the things they wash away, wash into the night and all the motors turn and turn—turn and turn until they cannot turn again. The wheel moves until it ceases to spin; stops where the movement reaches its end. And, all the days, all the nights, they crash into their unforgivingness; crash into their own inevitable end. The beginning of the beginning.

*   *   *

It was late now. The daytime light was dimming; city lights were coming on.

Off the bike; parked it by a supermarket, on a side street. We got in their car. We almost did not though. For it was a major shock to realize that we: S.J. and I, would have to sit in the back seat.

I mean this was just *no-go city;* something we never did. In his ride, I rode shotgun. In mine, S.J. did. But, the bike, (the bad dude), was down for the count; there was little choice in the matter. And, after all, two babes were at hand/in hand.

The drive was on. We drove off. *The Greatful Dead* played on the tape machine.

"Could you turn that shit off!"

They were naïve. They were young. But, they were obviously, very-very available/haveable.

We: S.J. and I, were young. We too were available.

So, I guess we found each other: the babes and us.

The two of them, they were B.H. kids. Beverly Hills—mega money/mega rich. We, S.J. and I were Hollywood dudes; street kids, raised in the gutters. They were they. We were we.

Discussion(s) seemed to lead to nowhere but nowhere itself. But the notable memory at the time was the fact that the driver discussed anxiety attacks—a person after my own heart, (or head), as it were at the time…

S.J. and the babe, side-riding, didn't know what she meant. We explained, the impending feeling of insanity, any minute, any second, coming on and on, coming down. Hell in the making. End of life/demise of humanity. Fighting to stay sane, when there was no-way/no-thing to battle. Overtaken…

We explained it, but it could not be understood by the uninitiated. Like *secrets of a sect*, we immediately understood each other. Her; the driver and I.

As all children seem to profess, claim, they are party animals; that they can party too—these youngsters were no different. They wanted to join the ranks of long time inebriated, intoxicated, asphyxiated individuals, like S.J and I.

Words are cheap, however. They never seem to mean a goddamned thing.

In the bounds of Malibu, we pick up a bottle of our passion, (S.J.'s and mine), J.D.: *Jack Daniels;* whiskey so supreme.

Top it off, chill it down, we grabbed two sixers on the side.

Now, by this time, with the passage of the Malibu liquor store, it was evening, it was dark; they, the two young bunnies had the pier in mind. It was the pier that we went to, the pier in Malibu that is.

The intoxicants were stashed in our coats, S.J.'s and mine.

For on the bike, though it had been warm, this day, a coat is generally what you need to take the edge off of the embrace of the wind.

They were stashed. We were on the pier. The Pier. The one outside and further past that restaurant. I forget its name...

The pier was ours. We had it to ourselves. The gates to the night were soon closed behind us. The pier locked off.

Time had no usage. It was conquered. The alcohol was distributed. And, as expected, they, (the two babes), had trouble choking it down. The brew and the J.D. were gag city for the sweet young mega money, mega rich, B.H. girls.

To make a long story short, the basic get to know one another(s), try to impress each other, conversation(s) went on-and-on-and-on. It came time, where it was time, to hang one; suggested by the darker haired B.H. princess; complete with braces on her teeth, as I later came to notice. Now, I was all up for that and ready for that session as was the other B.H. babe in tow. We left the pier, and the bottle with S.J., who had no reason to leave his power spot of attention.

Through the restaurant, the pier gates, (now begin locked); across the street to the fast-food stands, onto its restroom we go.

Hanging one... When you really have to... Ah, it is heaven...

Done with our deed(s), back across the street, back through the restaurant; via the negative glances of all those, (oh so supreme people), who were dining, and the, (oh so great employees), waiters and waitresses, them all, who were serving the oh so supreme. I have to admit, it did make me feel a bit uncomfortable. But, back on the pier, S.J. in sight, the initial scene did not look too good...

He, S.J., was slouching on the bench. The bench where we had sat. The bottle in his hand and exposed—not concealed as we had kept it previously. Exposed and empty. Fuck!!!

We walk up,

"Hey man, what's going on?"

S.J. slurred, with the distant eyes he gets. They become more than Chinese eyed... More than, because he has Chinese eyes. They also become more than glazed, they become more than crossed, they become more than tilted. He was majorly fucked up! He had killed the remains—drank the majority of the bottle himself!

*   *   *

And, the distances grows as we all know, running, hiding, until it is hidden away. Nowhere to run is the only place to run and the poetry speaks of the screaming and the intoxicants hide the pain, and the rich they fall, and the poor they dream, and when there is no more use in pretending and no longer any reason why and when there is no more lies you can tell, no more dreams you can feel, and the moment it is lost forever; death it comes so easily.

*   *   *

The time to leave the pier was evident; evident and eminent.

"Let's go, man."

I spoke the words to the big, bad, and fucked up S.J.

"OK, Man."

So, he gets up as I laugh it off, to the more than alarmed B.H. babes.

Well, they thought they knew how to party... They thought they knew what partying was... They thought they knew... But, they didn't know shit! This was party to the maximum. He and I, S.J., we know this party well...

We: he and I, had been down this road before.

After I helped S.J. to his feet, I was more than a bit pissed for he had killed the bottle and where was I going to get my high from? In any case, we began to walk.

"I'm going to go for a swim."

I look over my shoulder and S.J. has climbed out onto one of the metal beams that support the lights which illuminate the surf, over the Pacific Ocean.

"I want to go for a swim!"
"Come on back in, man. That water is cold!"

The two young, supposed, party girls are there; freaking out. *"Calm down,"* I tell them.

In truth, I was not at all looking forward to the prospect of having to jump into the water to save the obviously way too fucked up Saturday Jim.

The convo. went back and forth between him and I for a while.

He wanted to swim…

Finally, I knew that discourse, and my telling him not to, would get nowhere; S.J. being in the state he was. So, I just got the girls and said let's leave. We began to walk away.

"See ya… I guess I get both of these fine young ladies for myself."

S.J. climbed back in. I walked back and helped him, to be sure there was no accidental fall—fall in the water.

We, the three of us, the B.H. babes and I, propped the bad dude up, as we exited to street level via the restaurant; with all its constituents of perfection gazing on. I had to give an extra little pull on S.J. as we passed the bar which he decided he wanted to have one; one bottle that is, for the road.

Truly speaking I, in my vague state of drunkenness, would have stopped, to intensify the dulling, fading feeling, as well. That is if they would have served us. But, with the underage babes in tow and them being our sole hope for returning to the confines of civilization—they had the car, you know. As such, exit seemed the only alternative.

We packed S.J. into the front seat. I, knowing him all too well, realized that he was sure to barf sooner or later on the ride back. And, if he is not in an available position, that is to the door, and if the car is not stopped immediately, he will sure as the sun is yellow in Van Gogh's paintings, puke all over the inside of the car. I know, because he has done it more than once in my ride.

This, I guess, is where the story really begins, or the beginning of the end, or something to that effect...

Now, I was university—ing in the valley. So, at the time, I lived in this fine little one-bedroom crib, complete with the pool, jacuzzi, and all, in Tarzana. S.J. was busy driving the big rigs, (well, actually the bobtails), so he lived in the city of our inception, destruction, etc; namely: Hollywood. The B.H. babes slightly enamored with this performance of partydom and it still not being past their bedtime/curfew, they were easily persuaded to drive up and over Malibu Canyon and into the great bound(s) of the L.A. San Fernando Valley—which I, even then, was embarrassed to say I lived in.

Now, with S.J. in the front fighting to stay awake, I in the back; well, in the back seems to be the best description. Dark and in the back. I mean it was night. And, up scoots next to me, and I do mean very next to me, this sweet young B.H. babe.

Now, to more fully describe the pair, (as I haven't really done that yet), she, the one next to me, was the youngest; fourteen as it turns out to be. Fourteen and with braces, brown hair and, in truth, not the one I was particular attracted to; though her features were a bit finer than the sandy blond drivers. Plus, her; the babe in the back seat with me, her touch was far more available.

She moved over as I sat—moved over close; very close. It was dark. It was night. It was the back seat. I could see the reflection of the driver giving continual glances, glances of wonderment, as to what was happening in her back seat.

We drove over the canyon. S.J. heaved once, three time, or so, but the ride went on. Me, I had a hand in my crotch, literally, a babe all over me. But, better judgment won out. Except for a few kisses, I kept my hands to myself. I kept the vision, desire, and mirrored reflection of the driver in mind.

We got to my apartment and in we went. S.J. headed over and onto the beanbag chair; the only actual piece of furniture I had in the living room and promptly proceeded to crash.

There I was left with two B.H. babes on my hands. We sat mid-floor, drank beer, they smoked cigarettes—something I normally never let occur in my pad. But, the mood was right, the further intoxication of my home supply of imported brews took hold, and after all, the night was young.

Now, let me put it this way; it was available—especially the younger of the youngsters. It could have gone, *wham bam thank you mame,* in pure threesome style. S.J. being asleep. But, I was not so tainted then. Not as tainted as I am today. And, as my main macho party friend was fast asleep, I could resort to the subject that took up most of my thought processes; spirituality.

Somehow back then, I guess eight or nine years ago, I allowed myself to be more dynamic, more in control of the conversive topic. Though dance, music, lust, and love, all were a part of me, they seemed far less valid than the call of the cosmic. Maybe I was more of a loudmouth back then. Maybe far less cynical. Maybe it was just closer to the time when I had left being a monk. I do not know? But, the discussion was placed in bounds of the mystical and as younger people are generally more influence-able or at least more tolerable/interested of a new and different subject, it did continue... The conversation of spirituality that is.

Maybe an hour into my discourse, S.J. wakes up, stands up straight as an arrow, lights up a cigarette, looks for an ashtray; not finding one, he simply tosses the match on the floor and bids his *adues*. He hits the trail. We all say, *"See ya."* It is not until maybe twenty minutes later: babes, boozes, discussions of cosmic consciousness, and all that I realize that, *"Wait a minute, S.J. lives in Hollywood, this is*

Tarzana, and he has no way home." The three of us go and look around the building for him: by the jacuzzi, by the inner park grounds, even in the parking lot. But, he has vanished.

We went back into my crib but their twelve o'clock curfew was quickly approaching. So, they went on their way. Me, I sliced my way to my van. Thought I hated driving drunk in the later hours of a Saturday evening, I went in search of S.J. I drove the streets to and from Ventura B.L.V.D. and even cruised it East for a ways... As far, that is, as I believed him capable of walking. But, he was nowhere to be found.

I returned home prepped up for the oncoming inception of the hang over I knew I would have—hit the before bed *alka seltzer* and aspirins and went off into dream land sure that S.J. had called someone and had gotten a ride home.

Next morning, up-and-adam, as it were; I put in a call to Saturday Jim. I get en route and in-line, his bro Venchinzo. S.J. was, out/asleep.

Venchinzo didn't know how he had gotten home but was sure that he was there. My mind to rest. I laid back, kicked on the tunes; relaxed and waited for the hang over. The hang over that never seemed to come. I was younger than...

The day went on and I got the call from S.J. in the early afternoon. His story went as follows: out my door, out the door of my apartment complex, out onto the street; walking... Past a liquor store, with a few bills in his pocket, he picks himself up another bottle of the Jack. He walked on. Hit Ventura B.L.V.D. Tried to hitch a ride but no luck in that direction; at least initially. Past a car, parked. Where this chick jumps out, followed by her dude who is screaming at her. She tries to get S.J.'s help/attention and grabs onto his arm. He tells her to fuck off.

Now, you have to understand this bad dude Saturday Jim, once he is placed in the party mode, he staggers, he falls, his eyes get crazy, and red, and tilt from one side to the other. When he is aced, he cares about little else. Babes notwithstanding. His mind is on living the intoxication. So, the babes... Well, they don't call him out.

He walked all the way to Laurel Canyon Blvd, which was five miles away. There, as he tells me, he took a little nap on the strategically placed fountain of the saving and loan on Laurel Canyon and Venture. Then, up and around again, he caught a hitchhiking ride over the canyon with some fag he had to jam up due to him trying to put his move on. The rest of the way was a walk down Hollywood B.L.V.D. which his crib lies just off of.

His story, not mine...

Later that day, we had to go pick up my bike; which was no easy accomplishment for neither one of remembered exactly where it had been placed. I motored over to Hollywood in the Dodge Motor Inn; my bad van type v— hack—al. We drove. We looked and looked, eventually to find it.

In the back of my van where a lot of stories have been lived; (some told, many of them untold); we pushed it in, up a wooden ramp. We moved it; my scoot, back to my crib, in The Val. And, that was that.

Evening rolled around and at ten o'clock a call on my telephone line. It was they, the babe(s), from the night before. A convo. ensued. Nothing much to tell. It was clear who was available and who was more in the romance league; if you catch my meaning?

A long story made short, as seems to be the preference of the times; she called me several time(s) over the next few nights. The older one...The one in the mode of romance.

Friday rolled around. I was a University student and a martial arts teacher at the time. Friday, that Friday, no—thing to do, no—one to call; (never been the first call babes). I was home. It was 9:00. I decided to get fucked up solo; play some music, watch some T.V. A beer or three down; *Dallas* on the television screen. The telephone it rings. B.H. babe on the line. The older one: seventeen; not fourteen. She wanted to come over. Come over with a friend; another friend/a different friend than the one the week before. She wanted me to go to the movies with them, midnight show, *The Fox Venice;* some stupid *Rolling Stones* flick to watch. With nothing to lose, everything to choose, AOK, I conceited.

They came over the hill. We sat back to a beer or three. The other, her other friend, even far more fine than she; a high school sweetie; B.H. just and all, still and all the same.

She wore Birkenstock sandals. I wore Birkenstocks; Birkenstocks and drawstring pants—still holding onto the yogi in me.

We sat. We spoke. We drank beer. The telephone rang, It was Ratso, a little space case of a drummer who played music with Saturday Jim and I. A loser by choice and content. He was way-way out there.

Hearing of the/my situation, he was full-on, on his short way over. I had the other chick meet him downstairs. I lived in one of those massive big apartment complexes, you know.

There he stood, or should I say, there she stood; several inches above his head. He was a short little guy... But, anyway and so on, we drank some more beer, had some convo., went to the movies; she my main B.H. babe at the wheel. She liked to drive...

We held our first hands than; that night, in the movies. We exchanged our first kisses than; that night.

S.J. Friday night story...

S.J., home and drunk, post his traditional Friday night black hooker session on Sunset B.L.V.D.

The next night, Saturday night, S.J. and I were out; no time for those pre—twenty—one-year olds.

But, as the week continued, however, the B.H. babe and I saw each other, a lot. And, we spoke every day.

There/with her, I could be, (I guess), more myself... But than, what is myself? I have/embrace both sides: the mystic, the drunk—continually dancing between the two. Both lead to enlightenment, I believe. Both are enlightenment, I know. With her, I easily/seamlessly dance between them; my two paths, my two roads—roads leading to the same place. She got it. She understood it. Very few people do. Most cannot grasp the subtlety of the understanding. Most people are of the world. Most people are of the addiction. Most people from that, drive down the road of the drink; and it leads them to devastation. Most people, not me; not her. We understood/embraced the subtitles.

The spiritual are too spiritual. If you claim to be spiritual, you are never spiritual; you just don't get it. You are claiming to be something—not being something. If you claim something, you never are. But, that is all another discourse(s). This one is about her— her and I.

We: her and I, talked; we exchanged passionate kisses. We didn't fuck. She was on the rag.

Then, came Friday; the next Friday. She came over early in the day. I had to go to the bank; Granda Hills, the closest branch. I lived by the 101 in Tarzana. A drive to nowhere, no— where but some—where fast for it was understood her blood flow had shut down, we were to have our first love—making session. This day/that day; today, a day that had finally come.

Maybe I was more clear back then, maybe more of a fool. Somehow/somewhere, on that ride, my mind decided about her; forget it!

Back to my crib, she pulls up for the park. I get out, *"See ya."* That was the last time I ever spoke to her.

Now, they say everyone has that one big chance in life, well maybe I blew mine. You see, her father was the vice president of one of the major television networks. I could have moved in and taken the ride.

I don't know... Maybe it was just that I was young, had the whole world in front of me. I still believed that I was to be all that I dreamed I would be. God, that was a long time ago.

Saturday Jim and I, well on Saturday, am I being redundant, we went out as usual; both our bikes working again and we did our traditional Venice drive, Westwood movies, and then to the place of choice; our favorite bar, with Cliff the bartender. And, as usual, we got way fucked up.

But, did I think of that girl; that night, (the young B.H. babe)? That night/a night I could have been with her. A night where we: S.J. and I, instead threw back a few dozen—a few dozen as people watched us in awh. A few dozen or more, as we had done so many times before. Did I think of her? Yes, I did.

But me, I chose the night. I chose the unknown. I chose the what was to come, over a young girl who loved me. I had made that choice before and I have made that choice again.

The darkness; riding drunk into the night, with the wind blowing through our hair... Our motorcycle scream below us as we encounter *Satori*.

A choice always has to be made. Then, you live with it.

At/from Saturday Jim and his wife and his kid(s)—my B'day dinner. The night/this night; not then but here. We're back to to-night.

Well, we chilled the day on and abouts at S.J.'s crib, drank our share of the brew(s); post the German movie/post his return from his labor and his dentist. PM rolls around. We dressed up in suits.

Well, me, I actually almost always wear a suit; a least a sport coat...

He, S.J., looks mighty Italian when he wears a suit. By the way, he is Italian.

Suited, we dinnered down. Younger days we would have gotten big time tilted; life and the aging alcoholic... But, we only got slightly titled.

Basic, semi—drunken discussion(s), we talked of the old days over dinner—talked for the ears of the other(s): his wife, his stepson, his stepdaughter, and his daughter, (my godchild). She's just a little girl...

Post the restaurant; post the reminiscences re-lived there, we continued the discussion; brought it into his car.

We talked of the old rides. Talked of the old nights, as we drove home.

S.J. drove; drove this night; drove us home; back in the direction of his crib. While driving, he says,

"This is the road we took that night. You, just out of the hospitable, after your motorcycle accident."

"Yeah, remember my hair was like this long,"

I signal a very short length, for they had shaved my head due to the brain surgery to take blood clots off my brain, in order to save my life.

He continued,

"I took him out and got him way fucked up, the second day he was out of the hospitable. What a low dude I was..."

I intercede,

"Yeah man, remember I thought I was seeing a UFO over there, up on that hill."

"Yeah, and it was a fucking fire, man! We were drunk!" He emphasizes the word.

I continue the convo...

"And remember we used to get so drunk in Westwood, that all the people at the bar would sit there in awh of how we could kill those bottles of Jack."

"Yeah man! And then we would walk out of there straight as an arrow and then have to carry each other the rest of the way to our bikes. That was back when we used to ride our motorcycles..."

I interrupt...

"Remember that time I was so fucked up every time I got on the bad dude to start it, I would fall off."

"Yeah, and I told you to be cool on the freeway man.

He turns to his wife in the back seat. *"And this guy takes off at a hundred miles an hour. I mean really; no shit! A hundred miles an hour. I couldn't even keep up with him!"*

S.J. looks to his wife as he details the details.

"Fuck, how we didn't kill ourselves back then is amazing." I question...

S.J. continues...

"Yeah, and then we get to his apartment and he had to have this pass key thing to get into the parking lot and he gives it to me and falls off of his bike. He's laying there on the mutha fucking street telling me I have to fucking chain up his bike and I'm so drunk I can't even see."

"Yeah man, but then you drove back home to Hollywood."

"Yeah, we were some party people!"

"Yeah, can't handle that shit no more..."

S.J. thinks for a moment and...

"Remember that time up there in Vancouver?"

"Yeah, you know, we used to go up there because we could drink at nineteen,"

I turn. I explain to his wife.

S.J. continues...

"One night, there's was some nigs, (his words, not mine), *making noise and sticking their heads out the window from the room next to us and this dude goes and puts a pillowcase over his head and sticks it out the fucking window. Man, we never heard nothing from them the rest of the night."*

"Yeah man, I fucking fell in your suitcase that night and wanted to sleep there. And, how about that time in Victoria, when I was so fucked up and driving, you had to tell me when the signal lights had changed colors."

S.J. continues the memory...

"Yeah and then we get back to our hotel and there was this stripper from the hotel bar down stairs, that we through some money at earlier

in the evening, and she wants to come and party with us up in our room. But, this dude is too fucked up! I have to carry him to the elevator and when we get to our floor, he fucking falls out the door of the elevator and is laying there on the fucking floor. I just about have to carry this guy to the room."

"Yeah man, that was the night I drank twenty— seven martinis…"

"Yeah, we fucking partied HARD. But, you totally fucked us up with that stripper, man. She just laughed at us and left."

We ride on for a moment or three… Basic semi—drunken discussion ongoing. We get talking about pussies and fucking; then, I say,

"It's different when you fuck chicks who have had kids, you can't ram in as well on that top wall of the pussy. I like that felling. It is the same, with chick who have had abortions; I remember this married woman, who I used to fuck. You remember her in that apartment building I used to live at out in The Val?"

S.J. shakes his head, *"Yes."*

"Somebody got her knocked up and she had an abortion…"

"Somebody, ha, ha, ha. Yeah, I know who somebody…" interrupts S.J.

"But, after that, I never could never feel the top of her pussy as well as I did before. What do you think, don't you think that is true?"

I started to sober up right then and I realized that I was rappin' all this shit while his babe, (the mother of three—plus, she had a few abortions of her own), was sitting in the back seat.

Fuck... I have one serious big problem of putting my stupid fucking drunken foot in my mouth around his babe(s). So sorry to her... I didn't mean it that way.

"No comment, big guy," was his answer, with a laugh on his face.

Post the *re-rendezvous* back at his crib—exchange of cars and all, I dove home, with all of my basic paranoia of another pop in the drunk driving CATEGORY. But, made it... And, here I sit/here I am.

The babe, my babe, you know the one, the main and current squeeze, left a message of direction to the place of her father's Monterey Park B'day party on the machine but no more message since then. Pissed no doubt... Embarrassed for sure, at my subsequent no show to a hundred dollar a plate dinner.

Remember, I bailed out of her birthday feast(s) of this weekend/on this day.

Family embarrassment. Chinese family. *'Quai—lo,'* no shows.

She thinks I have money; I don't. And it is hard to tell someone, (go into long explanations there-of), that you are zero; especially when all your proper senses tell you, *"Bail out!"*

Maybe she got my exit hint. Maybe, but I doubt it. She does not give up easy. It has been nine months of my exit stage left, but she will not let me go; no—no matter how much I beg, plead, piss her off, and bargain.

So, she is probably pissed. So what... Maybe she is out, cha—cha—ing around.

No, I know she is not. She is home brooding and, no doubt, I will get a call probably *manyana*. But, *manyana,* I have somewhere else to be; 9:30 AM.

Saturday Jim's love bucket's, first child, (his 1st stepchild), bicycle race in Bakersfield.

Saturday Jim, he and I will go up there TO—GET—HER.

But now, it is late, way late, my late; 3:30 AM. I will rise 8:30 AM; minimal sleep—ish. So, enough of this/enough of that. Enough story(s) told...

And me, I'm onto another dream...

...night—time FIVE

Mostly, my energy is zeroed. The stories of my life; the same... Perhaps best left for renaissance(s), when all things seem better, and less, seem(s) like more.

A day, a full day—a ride to Bakersfield. Bakersfield, California; about a hundred miles North/East. Saturday Jim's brown headed stepchild, won; shall I say he destroyed the bicycle race competition.

Adolph, the Destroyer. Dutch by mother, German by father, by birth and by bloodline; a true racing machine.

*   *   *

My next-door neighbor's screams, right now. It is late night. They are rude. They party down; life and where else do I go?

Mostly, I need to get away. Where and when is the money?

*   *   *

Back to the/this day...

The race sets up; the announcer states, *"This is for the senior category. The riders, with more expensive sunglasses than, category four."* He was making a joke...

The race; the stepson, he got his Andy Warhol fifteen minutes of fame. He deserved it. He seriously kicked all the other rider's asses.

They even interviewed me, his trainer... Interviewed by a more than appealing, bicycle-logical of a female journalist—thought I do not tend to like the wonder white bread flavoring; she is/was just the type of said that I would go for in a pinch/clinch. Even Saturday Jim said the same.

"I knew it," he exclaims. *"That is just the style of white bread you had up there in San Francisco."*

I thought about it for a moment, and though not exactly; as this chick was more Santa Cruz than San Francisco looking; yeah, there is/was a similarity.

Another girl/another time/another story.

*   *   *

The woman, the one discussed previously, the one mentioned before... No, not the said one of this moment of motion, at the bike race, but the main and current L.A. squeeze. She, now; right now, has called the machine. Good and bad. Obviously, she is pissed. As previously stated, maybe she will take the hint of my desired exit.

But, in fact, I hope that she is OK. I realize I probably chilled her bones very seriously on the serious side. No show, no-go again, to a family outing where I was expected. Where, I was paid for; a hundred dollars a plate.

Family embarrassment in a Chinese family; not an easy thing to conquer or cope with.

When I saw her last—last with her naked unconquered body, that morning; yesterday morning, God, it seems likes years ago... But, that's my life—I live so much in one day/everyday; everything seems so long ago. But, then/there something slipped, something like my soul, it was like a magnetism to her form, her form of control. Usually, I am instantaneously non—attached; here now and there-for it has taken me, to now, to even want to forget.

Mostly, let me put it this way, she upsets me so much, I wish I had somewhere, into some new illusion, to run.

She will call, her attachment is way far deep—usually a day of silence turns her into the monster of desire, but I wish that she would just leave me alone. There's no win in one of those/one of these situation(s).

In or out it is all a loss.

And though I spent a day of supposed recreation, three of my cameras in my hands, I am burnt/burned out; tired. And, though I suppose I could write more; a moment of nothingness/lost in the sleep may do more to/for the poetic form.

The neighbors they scream, they seem on the verge of fight. Life and its non—silence, when I would prefer to listen to the ocean waves; no fair.

But then, sometimes things are fair, fair and funny, like a disco night, maybe 1977, Saturday Jim and I were nineteen. Victoria, Victoria, British Columbia. Drunk out of our minds. I wore contact lenses for a month. What a hassle. Not worth it. One fell out. Saturday Jim, crawling around, found it on the pounding disco floor. He, S.J. told the story to Adolf today—Adolf, the destroyer. I had forgotten about it; that story—forgotten until maybe six months ago when S.J. had reminded me for the first time...

My telephone answering machine it is on to catch any incoming calls; if there are any more—if you know what I mean.

*   *   *

silence is golden
especially when it is not
your own noise
which is breaking the magic spell
the summer draws closely to an end
the fools
try to grab onto
the last remaining chance
at a seasonal party
that never really existed
in-thought and/of in-form

the night time
it is for whispers
whispers leading to the dream
dream of dreams
someplace to be
someplace
where all the winning is winning
all the chances are taken
and something comes out of nothing
instead of
nothing from something

give me a moment of silence
give me a moment to dream
give me a moment of fulfillment

for I have given many
pre-paid in return.

...FOUR

Decide, negotiate, calculate; she won't be here for at least an hour—4:14 PM, traffic and all. I have a painting to do, writing(s) to write. But, I have just a bit of time.

Paint, yes... I think I can and/or will write; if I have some time. The story to tell of love and lust; in its nighttime session.

And, no-one knows more than I, how I walk the razors edge of life; the tight rope over a fire lies right behind me, following close at hand, waiting to jump out at me.

And, no-one knows more than I, how I jump at ever chance for a glance at/of illusion. It is killing me, I know... Yet, I cannot, *"Just say, No."* The creativity is what suffers the most...

Post the Painting...

So-so at best...

I feel rushed, but than I often/always feel rushed. I have never learned how to just not care; how to do things with ease. The impending ~TIME DANGER~ is always chasing me, close at hand.

Now, as I have gotten older, my heart hurts, of late; blood pressure surges. Well, it often has; but the age, it has taken its toll, and death could be eminent with a hurting heart, a rushing blood serge, cerebral hemorrhage—my head did meet the pavement once, big-time; leaving it in no condition to take chances with...

Complain, complain, complain...

Illusions begin as they start, their downfall to their impending end.

Monday, today is Monday. I knew there was to be another *function at the junction* with the Chinese set of my bail—ing babe's fam—a—lee.

9:45 AM, ring me on the telephone line. I hear a voice, a voice from the not so distant past. Click, I hang up. The phone it rings again. *"Hello." "Don't hang up!"*

It was her. The call I knew that would be coming. Inevitability...

But, the/this story; this portion of the story—this particular writing, must halt. It all equals the same end, anyway...

Why must it halt? *She has arrived...*

...THREE

Dinner, it cost me two hundred twenty-five plus: a watch for her father, a floral arrangement for an uncle, gas, and time; a perpetual waste of...

Sex, this morning. Sex I did not want to have. Price for said sex; high.

A doghouse for a dog of hers which I do not even like, on my bill. Breakfast in the realms of big bucks. Me, with *danero* in the negative amounts; anxiety, inner pain, I still have to pay for everything. She still expects me to pay for everything.

Plus, in the PM, her past, was reminded to me again,

"Are you an artist?"
"Yes."
"She always likes artists."

So says an aunt or something in her description of her... Her; my main and current, L.A. *glam slam* babe. There at her father's third, (I guess), B'day party.

* * *

Dick list. Hers it is just too long. I knew it before. *Good girls don't but she does.* Her family has to remind me of it, again. Stroke her ego. She smiled when said words were said.

She yelled at me in the parking lot, as she drove off just now. Now, just a few minutes ago.

"What do you want me to do?"

It is 3:00 PM.

What I want, she cannot give. What I need, she hasn't got.

Me, a fool in his artistic loneliness, a fool, none-the-less.

I wish there was somewhere that I could go; go away. I have been trying to do just that for more than a minute; more than a little while. Money on the bad side. What is it that I can do?

She calls. I only do not answer for a few days. Addiction of the worst kind.

Addiction that I do not even want. A girl I do not even love.

Addiction, that kills for its thrills; so intimately connected that every action is either like the bliss of pure uninterrupted cosmic orgasm or the scream of a cold steel knife in the back.

In a place/space where the lost magic of any moment, the lost soul to the capture/rapture of a form, is too quickly shattered/tattered, in the oblivion of the nothingness.

I am getting too old for this.

Though she longs for me; though she gives up everything for me; too much has transpired, in too long a time, of the past; *good girls don't but she does.*

I don't ever want to feel this way again. Trapped, no way in, no way out.

*   *   *

Soon, I will get a phone call, for soon she will be home. I know because that's how it goes... She will say, *"I love you. I need you. I want it to work. Just tell me what I can do and I will do it."* I know for I have heard those words so many times before.

She will say, *"I love you!"* I will say, *"So what."*

Now, here I sit; here I write—energy at energy level zero. Fifty-six lines of computer type/melancholy hype.

> Give me another reason.
> Give me another chance.

Run, I could run. Sleep, I could sleep.

The nowhere closes in. The boredom of all the places I have been, one too many times. The frustration of the feeling(s), I have felt way-way too many times. Life...

Lies... Yes, I have told her a few. Addiction, it runs so deep.

> *No way in.*
> *No way out.*
> *Any dream will do.*
> *Scream for the dream.*
> *With every dance*
> *there is another chance.*

So, I have become waylaid late in the sense of a day of not writing; not writing too much. I guess the story, this story, needs to be told...

> a nap
> a telephone call,
> actually several
> telephone call(s)

she said the things
which I knew that she would say
two paintings,
I paint
above the so-so level
and here I am,
less than motivate,
more than the world closing in.
I play the power game,
she is to come back over.
Back over in a little while.
The nighttime is upon me;
should I paraphrase,
should I detonate.
Yes. I will.
Either one will do just fine.

...night—time THREE

8:37 PM. You know, I should have some better place to be. My upstairs neighbors are running, pounding, or something on their floor—my ceiling. The same old story, disturbed, upset, by the noise of others.

I feel like I have little room to maneuver, little room to complain, however; for you see the babe of main discussion, *in this text,* you know the partially main L.A. *glam slam* scenster of a babe. Well, she, she likes to yell. She likes to scream. It is really quite embarrassing.

Me, I only have two windows of light; both big, both sliding, both facing the ocean. My bed next to one; my living section, facing the other. And, thus and therefore, all the screams go right out the window, right into the ears of other(s); namely my neighbors.

Me, I am a quiet sort of dude. I don't like people to know my business. She is a no—care sort of person; fuck who hears, and fuck what they think.

Well, that is only a partial truth, for if it is at her West Hollywood crib, just up the street from *The Whiskey,* it is, *"Shuuuuu. Be quiet. Don't say that. I don't want them to hear."*

At the crib of this soulful dude, yours truly, however, it is way the opposite.

I remember once, not so long back, a week or three deep, that we were having one of our perpetual disagreements and I got up and she screams, *"Don't hit me!"* And, I do mean screams. This with a good percentage of my neighbors out on their Pat—tee—oh's, Bal—con—knees, as it was a warm, sunny day.

Now, let's get down to the basics here; I have never hit her. Some of her lame dudes of the past have not been so kind, and she still flinches whenever I move my hand or arm quickly. Now, this pisses me off; about as much as the amount of dicks that have been in her pussy. As it seems like, in all counts, her past is continually chasing her (and me).

It/I have not always been so nice, however. There have been a few women that have met, Mr. Hand, if you know what I'm talkin' about. But, time, age, tempering, maturity; call it what you will, I have not been driven into that level of wrath with her; though she has deserved it far more than the other one(s) who I have not been so nice to. Still, she screams... Screams at something I have never done.

Once, back a time ago, us in bed, windows open, she begins rapping about far less worthy men. Ex's if you will. Men, other than I.

It came close; believe me, when she did that post a serious lovemaking session, and the supposed magic that took place... Then, for her to bring up other dudes; even if she was expressing, to your truly, they weren't as good as me—had smaller dicks than me, had saggier balls, and/or couldn't fuck her as long or as hard as I can. I mean, I already knew all that... But, before I had the full-on inclination and blew up, I was rising to get out of bed, to just walk away. But, as I did, she screams than she yells, *"Stop hitting me!"* Something I had not even done. Now, this was in the late spring, Sunday afternoon; everybody was out.

Well, what can I say? I imagine their, (my neighbors), opinion(s) of me are not so high. Damned by something I didn't even do.

So, I feel stuck/trapped/fucked even in my own place. Due to her words, her screams, her misdirected/false accusations—as such, and because of which I can't even complain about people bip-boppin upstairs.

Screaming, she always does that. A day; a few months ago—out in my parking lot; she was yelling and I just wanted to drive away... She didn't want me to, however. So, she grabs a hold of and rips off the new con—vert—a—ble top on my *Jeep;* ($649.00), forcing me to stop. With me stopped, she yells and screams to everyone's ears, then tries to kick me as I attempt to remove the remaining portions of the *Jeep's* top; now laying on the pavement. Myself, being a Martial Art(s) Master Instructor had no problem intercepting the oncoming kick with my foot. But then, top of her lungs, *"Stop kicking me!"*

Anyway, I suppose this is all funny, (at least in a certain light). But, when there is no place to run and all eyes are on me, it does not feel that way.

I could get into the psychoanalytical perspective of her need to scream; a method of getting her own way, as she was a very spoiled, mega-rich child; one of the only full-on limousine families, back there/than in Taipei. But, that means nothing to me... This is NOW, that was THEN. This is my life, here in the now, that she is fucking up.

One might ask, *"Why am I with her?"*

Well, I am trying not to be, as I have mentioned more than once or thee-hundred times in these pages. I have attempted this since day one.

One of those things, you know...

I even attempted a bail session to ASIA, (as I detailed). But, as karma would have it, back in L.A.; *Rose Bowl Swap Meet*, who do I walk face-to-face into; no lie. A million fucking people, going a million directions and she walks directly into me/I into her...

I tried to bail; just kept walking. She wanted to know, *"Why?"*

I walk. She shows up at the crib an hour or so later. And, it has go since then.

Lies, Money, Power-Trips, like the oncoming to-night.

The fool I am. The addicted, alone, artistic fool that I be.

*   *   *

time tick
the clock ticks
all I can write about
is my own life

fiction is for fools
fiction is for the non—lived
I would rather hear
the whoos of another

than read the lies of authors
in literary heat

hours go
life is lived
what is it all worth

a poem here
a painting there

time ticks
hour(s) tick
I am no better off
than I was a moment ago

older
I am just older

*   *   *

The telephone rang yesterday, 9:45 AM. I answered it. It was her, my semi—main L.A. babe. She cried her tears, where had I been. Out, I had been out...

Push comes to shove and any illusion will do. Then/there, back there I was still lost in that momentary soul snatching that I had felt a few days the previous; of her form, neatly locked into mine. You know, I wrote about it...

It is sad how short-lived illusions are— how quickly the lust of a fool fades.

West H'wood; my destination. We lay in her bed awhile. She was, not in, *'the mood,'* "I am embarrassed. I am hurt," so she states. You know, my not showin' up at all. Two times; times two—two of the B'day parties. Her father's not mine.

Love wrapped up in the blanket of nothingness. Actions they speak louder than words.

A love touch here, a love touch there. I changed her mind. We experienced minimal lovemaking.

*   *   *

A loft, she wanted me to rent her/us a loft; a downtown loft, $950.00 a month.

No actually loft, *"But you can build us one."* So, she said.

No actually kitchen, *"But you can make us one."* Fuck that...

It pisses me off, all the things I could do for her/for us. But sorry, I do not want to live downtown, in the pseudo hip bullshit environment that everyone now thinks is so goddamned artsy.

Old building(s): cockroaches, rats, criminality, and impending violence; all while paying top dollar to live in said. Live in said, with no kitchen. *"You can make us one..."*

But than, she is that kind of person; full-on, to believe the lie.

*   *   *

We were en route to getting lunch, I turned around and took her home. *"FUCK OFF!"* Were my words.

As she walked from my car, I saw that vision of innocents she keeps so well hidden beneath all of her layers of tainted-ness. There were tears in her eyes.

Nice guy. I am too much of a nice guy. I began to drive away. I could not go. Back in; into her parking spot, walk down the path, up the stairs to her apartment, *Number 6;* knock, knock. Apologies made. Hugs, hugged. I left again but left with grace and peace.

As I drove from her driveway, she was walking/passing, video to return, to the near-by video rental store. I picked her up. Let her back in the car. We set out for lunch again. But, this time, she paid my bad little, *'64 Porsche 356 SC,* an unwanted complement. She stepped on a newly painted red curb as she entered. She brought some of said red paint into the car, on her shoes. She placed it neatly upon my newly carpeted car. Fuck me again! Do you know how much that carpet cost? Fuck me for being a nice guy!

Lunch, it was Greek, over on La Cienega. I don't really like it there. Thirty—five dollars down, plastic painted upon my cerebral walls. I am taking her home, she starts in, *"Why did you have to do that on Saturday? Why didn't you show up?"*

You know, my dinner with the Saturday Jim...

To be continued...
She, the babe has arrived.
I wrote while awaiting her arrival.

...night—time TWO

Distraction/attraction, leave it to me to let myself be swept away into the arms of desire. Leave it to me to let myself be taken in; into the abode of the demon goddess of lust: so pervasive, yet so stifling. Like wishing, I had done more, created more; I don't want that to be the last feeling I have when this life comes to a close.

Desire lost in time; lost where any dream will do.

*　　*　　*

do you have it
I will take it
take it for whatever it is worth
do you know it
can you show it
love, lust, passion, sex, anything at all

can I take it
will you give it

the price
it is never quite clear

lost to the love of loving
when you really don't want
to love at all

lost to the realms of desire
when you really don't care

give it to me
I'll take it
        whatever dream
        you have to offer will do

you see, I am a seeker
one in pursuit
of any way in
        which leads to any way out

a reason for me
        to lose the pain
make it go away
        if only for a moment
take it from me
        if only in your dream
and speak to me
as others have spoken to me

lies
I want to hear your lies

*   *   *

Forever, I continue to torment myself, with letting the, *'call out,'* call me out. Then, looking around seeing nothing was accomplished I simply become more than upset with myself.

The *call out* today, it took me up and over, into the city, the city where *The Heat* is much more high. I came, I saw, I... The bike shop where I had picked up this new *Bottecchia* bicycle frame a week or two the previous; closed—*Yom Kipper* today. Whatever that is.

Thus, and so forth, and so on, it wasn't open; meaning a journey *manyana;* (as they were to put new a new *groupo*—components on it for me; *Campagnolo Super Record*...

But then, the journeys are what always seem to hold the answers; at least they seem to dangle the keys of temptation.

San Francisco, what was it? Maybe a bit more than two months ago... *Museum of Modern Art:* art opening, gallery showing. It was bad, not good. I, I had proceeded to get a wee bit too tilted prior and previous to the eight o'clock arrival time on the scene.

Come to think of it, I had juiced down a bit on the hard side the night before in SC, (Santa Cruz), as well. There, as here/SF, (San Francisco), it had been on the I—tral—yan side: pasta, minestrone, red wine, and the such...

There, SC, I had gotten a bit tilted, turned around on my way back to my love crib; with my lonely love pud in hand. I made it though; no duce, to inhibit my route.

The next night, post my drive to the city; that city, SF, not this city, L.A. I hit it on the I—tral—yan side again at this little *restaurante,* that I more than dig, up in the *Gay Bay,* over on Polk Street.

Polk Street, faggot central. Young men selling this ass's out on the street. Not to different that Santa Monica B.L.V.D. down here, L.A. way.

But and well; re: the gay boys—all of SF certainly has a percentage of that gender roaming around. That gender, if you can call them that.

Anyway, I dig this little place. I found it a few years back one night when I was out on the streets looking for appropriate dinning. Come to think of it, it was the night Geraldo, opened the vault of Al Capone, *"Live, on National Television."* Remember that fiasco?

But, that is another story/another time. This little *restaurante* though, has outdoor dining, some really good red *vinos* from Italia, etc. and anyway. And now, the owners and the waiters all dig me.

Me, I ate there, as I always do—up there in the SF.

So, that was the beginning of that night. THE BEGINNING...

After, I cruised on back to my *Hilton* hotel crib, room 30 *bla-bla-bla* something; java downed a bit via the in—room java maker; kicked back to some SF T.V. and awaited the moment of motion.

I have stayed there more than a few times. There has been a memory or three lived there—plus, memorable movies watched, sketches drawn, and loves lived with love(s) that have come and gone...

Generally, I head up to *Gayasia* (SF) about once a month. Distraction being my desire and all. In—fact, I feel more than ready; right now/right at this moment, to make that drive. North? Maybe...

It is almost funny, for I, at that time APPROX. two months ago, had just returned from the mega Five Star world I live in/within in Asia—only the best hotels will do. Then/ here in the States, I general am far more aware of my expenses, and my impending financial doom; limited credit card remaining balances, and the like. Thus, and therefore, I try to chill it back a notch and keep the out-going *danero* down.

That last trip to SF, in fact I had not planned to crib there at *The Hilton* but hit this little *Travel Lodge* I have stayed at more than a few time over on Polk. You know, kept expenses down... But, it was mid-summer and the cheap(er) rooms in SF, they were hard to come by. So, for whatever it was worth, that was my base, *The SF Hilton.*

In fact, that hotel serves a dual purpose for it is in walking distance of both my little I—tral—yan hangout as well as that of the aforementioned museum. Walking distance, if you're willing to walk a bit—which I actually like to do.

So, there I was: my room: red walls, used and abused; gold bed spread. I could hear people walking/talking in the corridors and the traffic, (sounds of the streets), invaded my space as it went by. This is *Gayasia*. This is SF. It is always so fucking noisy in the day/in the late afternoon.

You know me, I like silence. Somehow it has not been my karma to receive it, however. So, for whatever all this/that is worth, I have picked up a pair of shoot your gun, save your hearing, headphones, which often accompany me on my journeys.

I first got the idea from that movie, *Jewel of the Nile,* when Michael Douglas' babe in the flick, Kathleen Turner, wrote her love novel(s) in New York City with them on. But, anyway... Silence, I long for it.

With the headphones on, still a nap was not possible; the noise vibrated within the room's small walls—even within the sought after silence of the, *save your ears from the gun shots at the shooting range*, headphones. It closed in. I went for a walk on, *The Streets of San Fransisco.* He, Michael Douglas, was in that too; remember? Probably not...

Down and around, the late afternoon felt good. Somehow it all felt like an offering to the goddess of SF: the movement, the observation, the incoming knowledge of the streets.

A few miles and a frozen yogurt later, I was back; back at the hotel, in preparation for the night.

Dark, now it was dark. Outside, I walked. Black suit on; a suit I had designed and had made up in B'kok. Remember that story? A storyline a week or two the previous to this storyline...

Black suit, black shoes; big and bulky, obtrusively ridged soles. Time, it was by *Cartier*. The new one I had recently picked up, S'pore at this *Rolex/Cartier* dealer where they love me.

I was in. The paintings sucked! I chilled my bones walking around, as the comments were made, *"This looks like this. This looks like that"* Noise, just fucking noise. Shut the fuck up!

Then/there I came upon this lonely young lass. White, wonder white bread. Though not my first choice in women and desire, but, I was in a space of *any dream will do.*

I pulled up, parked it next to her. The enormity of the white walls and the hundred-foot-high ceilings dwarfed the paintings that were to be viewed. She stared deeply into one, deeply as she swayed back and forth.

"What do you think," she inquired.
"Essence, the essence is interesting," I answered.

As the crowds moved around us, we stared; time it ticked to the non-contentment of the moving masses.

The art was shit. But, I had no better place to be than standing there next to this chick, who was dressed in white tights and a mini skirt and who would occasional sway her way into me and periodically glance in my direction with eyes appearing to be dilated to the max.

Let's put it this way; *Hey, this is San Francisco, and the chick must be duped up on acid.* You know, with all this fucking bullshit sixties revival going on and all...

A hour passed, the museum was to close, up pull this salt and pepper couple; she white, dyed blue *do*. I mean come on, which way to the seventies? He, black; looking Africana; both sprouting leathers.

"What do you think it looks like?" Was the question she asked me.
"What do you think it looks like?" Came the answer I gave her.

Eventually, she, the white and blue *do-ed* chick, went into the discussion of how she thought it had the form of a woman with her legs spread apart. She made these statements while looking me dead in the eyes.

I mean hey, alright, I know I'm a babe and she was obviously warm for my form but she had *El Negro* in tow and I do not go that route. I mean, I'm not into interchangeable love and all—especially when it involves another dude. And, I mean hey, I got this duped up chick here/and on the line.

So, they shut down the factory. I had to pry my LSD'ed friend away, who claimed she was looking for just one more answer in the painting before she left. Sure... Yeah right... Whatever...

We headed down the elevator with the salt-n-pepper team. I had to guide my new-found lust acquaintance once or twice towards the door, because she kept getting distracted by whatever weird visual seen she was seeing. She was seeing stuff that no one else was privy to.

But, we made it out. Out onto the street. There, we parted company from salt, pepper, and blue—that hair—do had an existence all its own...

They climbed onto a scoot, like a Honda or something, and they were off into the night; alright. I am sure she fucked her Africana real good that night and fantasized it was me.

"A woman with her legs spread open..." Remember?

The acid-bound chick; her and I... We felt the night heat of the street, stared for a moment at a bus stop, pit stop of a glass wall, saw within its bounds a memoir of the SF symphony.

The SF duped up babe motioned to the effect that she would be singing for them. Singing for the symphony?

We stood, we stared for a moment more; me lost in the night glare of what I felt to be a LSD contact high and all, than moved in the direction of South—down towards the downtown, the worse-er side of San Fran—cis—ko.

And I mean hey, *if you're going to San Fran—Sis—Ko be sure to wear some flowers in your hair.*

We passed this bad bro who asked for a little bit on the spare change side of the picture, *"Sorry bro, nothing in that de—part—ment tonight."*

It was a funny sensation, he made a comment about me being with and/or attempting to get some pussy off of the babe; duped up as she was, in tow. I laughed. It was like instant camaraderie. I don't know how can I say it, me being the white boy, honky who spent the first ten years of his life growing up in South Central—somehow I just relate to the low-life of the/on the black hand side. It is like seeing somebody from some long lost past land; distant brotherhood. Or, should I say, bro—hood. Any—way...

We moved down South. South down Van Ness. She didn't like the vibes, so we turned and chilled it back Northward, past the bro—

ham again; comments and smiles it tow. We than sat down upon the steps of the symphony hall, had a little convo—sation.

She almost seemed normal, almost came down to earth for that moment. She looked beautiful, white bread beautiful. One of those chicks you look at one way and they are AOK, and then look at them again/another way and you see semi—uck.

She bound from Des Moins, Iowa. Hey, *Locals Only,* in my book. Born in California, (or Asia) or you weren't born anywhere.

But, post all that basic bullshit, she tried to tell me her name, a name that I did not want to know.

Saturday Jim, he always tells me, tells me that I come on too strong.

"I'm speaking serious matrimony here!"
"I'm the one that you have been waiting for all of your life!"
"So, you must be totally in love with me by this point..."

Three of my most used lines. And, etcetera...

This time, to A—VOID any complications, I said *nada.* When she tried to tell me her name, *"I don't even want to know it,"* were the words from my lips...

We decided to move on down, past the point of no return, and hit a little restaurant, IHOP, (The International House of Pancakes), WT, (White Trash) central, over there on Lombard Street. Her idea, not mine...

Obviously, she was from the Mid—West with ideas like that one.

But, my car lost deeply in a hotel parking lot and SF being a much more walked city that L.A., it was foot travel in mind.

We walked on... The conversation it was distant, she being duped and all.

The night it had cooled; cooled as only the summer night(s) of SF can. Cooled just right.

We walked past *The Hard Rock,* tourists as in every city lined up to get a table. Fuck that! I don't even like the place(s).

We moved on, past a little high—tech, nuevo hip piano bar of a singles bar; negatory comments were made on her part so we moved on.

A little farther down, she commented to the effect that she had changed her mind about going to IHOP. *No problema,* I didn't really want to go there anyway.

There was some passing notion that we should go up and back to her place, AOK, that was what was on my mind anyway.

Now, these comments and notions were cryptic at best—she being this stoned little chick and all. But, I could play along... I mean hey, I had been duped once or thirty myself, way back when, and though I now think acid is one of the worst things that anyone can do to their brain; I suppose Dr. Tim could argue the opposite. Anyway, I could play it off.

On our way back, the other side of Van Ness; still tripping, she made the motion of emotion to let's hit that little singles bar/piano bar. *"OK, let's do it."*

As we crossed the street, she began to relate this story, (a warning if you will), of how her, *"Boyfriend,"* who now, incidentally, was latched up at the love shack with his past babe of a girlfriend... In any case, apparently, he had kicked the ass of the last love stallion he had seen her with. Her, the duped up wonder white bread of a chick. *"Bring the punk on,"* I said. *"It will be fun to watch him fall."*

I mean come on! Why do chick(s) always pull that shit? They always want to impress the new dude on the line with what their past love stud was capable of doing; be it money, fight, or fame. Anyway... We hit the place.

We're chillin' down upon these couch type seats, the love being perpetual in its motion and all. The piano to our stern; the bar, (single, as it may be), to our aft, and the drinks they were in motion. Hers, a *Mai Tai;* mine a mineral water.

We lay around in all that loving bullshit. Her leaning against me. Listing to an occasional mis—played note upon the old ivories. And, the night worn on...

She leaned over to me, eyed dilated as all hell, place the back of her head upon my shoulder, turned slightly, and gave me a kiss. The best of the first kisses to date! Wet and wild in all of its fading duped up glory. I knew where this evening was going to lead...

Post another *Mai Tai;* keep them drunk you know... Paid the bill AMEX platinum. We were packing to leave, as the door approached, *"I think that's him, I think he is following us!"*

She looks to some guy walking out on the street in the shadowy, dark distance.

I have to admit it, her statement, did ruin the lust of the moment... But, *"Bring the punk on!"*

I mean now, come on... There hasn't been a guy I couldn't handle with my hands, feet and/or legs yet. Plus, I had my bad, in the pocket, butterfly knife to take off the lose edges of any confrontation that might befall this bad young pup.

I related this story to Saturday Jim, post and after. He states, *"Yeah, some fucking Gay-Bay Maricone is going to take you on... Good luck."* Him and I, in our day, (which is still present), being some seriously bad, street fighting *hombres*. We both laughed.

We, her and I, walked out the door and maneuvered in the direction of her pad; up and off of Polk Street. No dude. It was just one of her paranoid hallucinations.

Her building, nice enough. The apartment, a fucking rat hole of a small single; complete with a black cat, who wanted out. I would have to say that the size and the smell of that place, immediately made me think to just fucking leave. Size-wise, the kitchen and the living room occupying about ten-by-ten in terms of square footage.

But, I entered the realm of hoped-for pleasure. We sat back on her foam pad that pulled out to a bed, exchanged a few kisses of momentary passion; none of them living up to that of the first. She said she had a sore throat, offered me a throat lozenge.

"Does it have acid in it?" I ask.
"I knew you were going to ask that."

Just in case, I didn't take it just the same.

Then she was up, a telephone call to make. Her love DUDE, (you know the one she spoke of), on the other end of the line. Again, there she was back down to earth, not the spacey acided chick of the museum/of the walk.

They rapped the basic bullshit. He apparently was on the fringes of suicide. Good, get rid of the losers of this world.

They exchanged loving comments. She said, *"I don't want you to hurt yourself,"* and all that bullshit. Then, she mentioned, she was with a friend; my first thought was, *'Oh... This is a payback—him with another chick, etcetera—a—mundo.'*

Basically, I had planned to bail, post her convo, and forgo the pussy. It was just getting too fucking weird and complicated.

Me, I was going to be a gentleman and wait for her call to end.

The cat, I did not dig. The chick and her bullshit, I did not need. And fuck all this LSD induced melodrama.

Off the phone, I was in the mode of bail; she, however, was all over my form. What can I say, the hormones took hold and what's a guy like me supposed to do?

She had this rather sculpted body. Tall maybe 5'11." Buff. She must have worked out. Red hair, under her arms. I commented... She said, *"Not always."* I said, *"It should be always. It is just the way I like it."*

Reddish brown hair upon her permed head. A not so full bush of a beaver; brown, w/ a touch of red. Boobs, on the small side; *no problema*. My dick in motion before I knew what was happening.

"Do you want me to wear a rubber?"
"Do you have one? If not, I have some."
"I have one."

I mean hey, don't jump out of an airplane without a parachute. As the Boy Scouts taught me, Be Prepared.

We power thumped. Nothing too exciting, except for the fact jack that her fucking cat tried to get in on the scene; kept climbing on me.

She came. I didn't. The problems with the entrapment of the bad plastic passion of the rubbers and all...

It seemed I was expected to crib for the night. Now here I was, still jetlagged, back less than a week, (from ASIA), tired from my no nap day, my no sleep last night, and cribin' in this hell hole of a nowhere place with a fucking cat that kept trying to sleep on my face.

Cum. I may as well cum.

"Lets take a chance."
"OK."

The sword re—drawn, I mean the pup was a little tired, fucking for an hour or so; Asia jetlag and all...

Asia, where *The Heat* is the causation factor of the purest form of circulation. I am in my best shape there. SF and the cold, well it was almost a decided upon notion to get *Dirty Harry* back in form.

I mean, *Dirty Harry,* he takes no prisoners. So many chicks knocked up, that Saturday Jim titled the bad dude, *Dirty Harry.*

In other words, I shoot no blanks.

So, its time to get it done now. Thus, ridin' raw dog; no rubber.

Me, I got its action done and completed. Nothing all that great. No mystical experience to write about. Just blew my cookies. In the process, the chick off again; maybe twice. She went to sleep. Me, I had a fucking black cat continually trying to sleep on my jetlagged face all fucking night.

The morning rolls around. I rose to find something pretty damn scary. The chick, well... She still had that dazed look in her eyes. Not a good sign, big guy. Not a good sign at all.

That AM I called my answering machine, at home, to check into the messages. But, keep that in mind for a second or two...

We, her and I, took a bath, in her bathroom. In fact, it, her bathroom, was about the same size as the rest of her *apartmento.* She did me right... Right, like a woman should do. Right, like all women in Asia do. She washed me down with a loofah, washed my hair in the tub w/ some cheap drug store shampoo. We power thrusted one more time in the tub; again nothing to write home about.

While doing all this, she kept rappin' these distant tales; eyes still in the clouds. I did not like what that implied.

I wanted to bail. I wanted out. But, it was not going to be that easy.

Post said session, we moved in the walkable direction of my rented hotel crib. Inside, changed from the B'kok black suit I designed, to my B'Kok green suit I also designed. Black, thick, saw blade soles, (you know the kind the cops used to wear), still intacted. Cartier changed over to a steel and gold *Rolex*. The in—room java maker, still on. Thought I was to be a cribb'n there that night/last night. The coffee burnt to the bottom of the pot.

My Arrival, none too soon...

I shot a few pictures of her, just for memory sake. I had left my camera(s) there. There in my hotel room. Nothing to brag about; she looked uglier on film than in person.

When I have looked back at them, her eyes still far away and distant.

In my Jeep, we cruised over to *Ground Zero,* a uck little place, I don't really like in *The Haight.* She ate. I had a cappuccino.

Into this discourse, she went. In the form of the purest poetry, it sounded a lot like the words I have written. I almost wished I would have pulled out my pocket tape recorder and got it down for posterity. But it, the thought of my tape recorder, had not come over come me by the time I had realized its art/the art of/in her words.

She spoke to the effect...

"He rode into town, motorcycle black, his clothing black. He came on a wind from the south—west or maybe it was from hell. I do not know? His skin matched the colors of the burning ambers; black, yet not quite black. White, yet far too distant, lost in the black to

be white. He held her body close, deeply into the night. He was large/full; clean, yet almost dirty. He took possession of a woman soul that night, drove her into the visions of hell. It was for a night, it was for a moment, it was for a lifetime, never to let her go; he would never let her go. Then he was gone. Gone with the female's soul in tow. He was gone, never to be seen again. Riding off into the wind of which he was born, of which he came. Gone forever."

"Do you understand me," she asked.
"I understand."

Mostly, I was understanding that this bitch was seriously burnt. Though there was a part of me, (a small part), that, for a moment, actually thought that I could save this woman. No, fuck that! Exit, I wanted out. But out, it is not always at hand.

So, we drove up to that place above the ocean, overlooking the old bathhouse. We watched the nothingness of the fog pass into oblivion. We spoke of life's nothingness and the etcetera.

Again, for a moment while sitting there with her, I actually thought that I might be able to help her. Help her gain control of reality, of her mind. I gave her a spiritual/mental technique or two to practice. But, it didn't/would not/could not help.

For a moment I thought that I... For a fool's moment I believed that I... Never mind!

Then/there, I realized that hanging with a fucking nut is a way far no-go situation. But the joke, in the secondary *depatmento,* is that I had recently actually been thinking of going and picking up another Master's Degree in Psychology. Fuck that! I don't want to deal with fucking nuts!

I wanted to bail but she was not allowing me to bail easily, however and the etcetera. As such, we spent the day, such as the day was, it was spent.

Evening began to dawn. The lights began to dim. We headed back to my little I—tral—ian stomping grounds for dinner and a bottle of the imported vino.

What this situation actually was; was getting expensive. Me with thirteen thousand dollars of travel bills coming in from my last jaunt to Asia and "I" acutely aware of the fact that "I" was in the negative category in the bank account department. Me, I was not particular enjoying all this spending. Especially, since I had already hit the pussy. And hit it, more than once!

As we sat there, she discussed how she had an audition in two days for the SF symphony, choir section. *"You must practice. I will just get in your way." "No,"* she said. *"You can help me. You are a musician, right? So, you can accompany me on piano."*

Fucked again! I guess that wasn't my way out.

The evening had come upon us, becoming summer it was late but not yet fully dark.

Back at her crib, I drilled her one more time for the old gip. Then, there she was naked, I got my clothing on. *"Well, I've got to go now." "What!!!"*

The chick, fucking freaks out on me. There she was standing with her back against the door, her arms outstretched, blocking my exit. Doing this while screaming at the top of her lungs about, *"How could I leave, with her naked? How I could I leave, after what I had meant to her?"* I mean, this was some serious fucking, Clint Eastwood, *Play Misty For Me,* shit. I thought I was going to have to duke my way out of the crib; she being big and buff and all.

Finally, after several confrontations with her screaming at the top of her lungs... I mean, I wonder what the neighbors think of her? But finally, I convinced her I just wanted to go out and get a *Jolt Cola*. Naturally, she wouldn't let me go alone, but I got her to chill a bit and to get dressed.

But then, the bitch couldn't decide what to wear. So, that went back and forth for more than a few. Finally, outside... Fuck... Damn, I love outside!

So, I motored right on over to my ride. There was no fucking way in the world that I was going to go through anymore of that shit. Then/there it came down again. *"I though you were just going to get a Jolt Cola! I want you to stay!"* Etcetera into infinity.

Now she, is fucking screaming, while these SF cops are down the street doing something. Figuring that if they heard her shit and came up this way, they may try to lay some blame in my direction. Blame for what, I pondered. She's a fucking psycho!

I again tried to calm her down; told her I had something in L.A. that I had to do the next day, which I had previously forgotten, and that I would come back in two or three days or she could come down and visit me.

At the top of her lungs,

"I don't have your telephone number! I don't know where you live!"
"Don't you remember, I left you my card."
"WHERE!"
"On your table."

Well, she didn't believe all that and wanted another. Luckily, I had some of my Thai business cards with me so I pulled out one of them. I had hoped she wouldn't notice that there was no telephone number on them, just my P.O. Box. Unfortunately, this was not the case. No problem... I wrote down a false phone number, with promises of calling and being with her. Calling her, the chick, who I did not even know or care to know her name. Remember S.J.'s warning and all?

Finally, I was in the car and out of there with her screaming after me. So, Saturday Jim was not necessarily right about keepin' it casual.

Fuck, by this point it was late. I motored on down to a *Motel 6* off the 101 in SJ, (San Jose).

Funky little dives, I don't like 'em. Low Class, (in a deep baritone voice). But, with Asia jetlag fever and all, I checked in. I needed some sleep. Remember, I got virtually none the night before with the fucking black cat trying to sleep on my face all night. *"That means he loves you,"* so said the girl... Whatever...

I checked in, packed-full of all my paranoia(s) of what she may or may not do in regards to my false telephone number, our sexual contact, the police, the mental ward, her shrink, (if she has one), and the so on and the so forth. But, at least; out of there, I was...

Back down in the South Bay of L.A., I told my friends over at the music store/studio, of my SF exploits. Them knowing of my usual abnormal women, just laughed at my continuing/ongoing dilemma.

But, it was not over...

A few days later I began to receive letters from her; which I am still getting now. Now, three months later. Letters of love, needs, psychopath—dom, poetry, and the so on. There was even a night, a late night, a couple of months back—god it seems like eternity... I was O.D.ing on coke and I even called her. I needed someone to talk to. But, that purpose being served, I never wanted to speak with her again. This, however, was not the case on her end, for when her phone bill came in...

Remember the fool calling his answering machine to check his messages from her crib?

With the bill in, my number in tow, she began her conversation(s) with my answering machine and occasionally with me. This of course came to a sudden end, as I changed my telephone number, (again), for about the fifth time in this year.

So, that's the story of her. All except the fact of the main and continually mentioned L.A. babe of/in this dissertation, who I had passionately/inadvertently bumped into at the *Rose Bowl Swap Meet* and passed a bit of a love disease onto her. Gotten, almost no doubt, from this SF nut case. Well, it may have been picked up somewhere in Asia Central. But???

Anyway, I did what any good, normal red blood American dude, would do. I blamed the main L.A. Squeeze. *"You gave it to me!"* Though, of course, it is apparent she has touched no one, save for me, even in my Asian absence. But...

I guess back to her, after a bit of a long deviation, hun?

*   *   *

"So, why did I have to go out to dinner with Saturday Jim, his wife, his stepdaughter, his stepson, my godchild, in tow? Because it was my only chance at a birthday dinner. The thought it was so special! They, the married ones, have never done that for me before." So, I told her.
"See, it really does matter to you. You try to act so fucking macho, you pretend that nothing ever bothers you. You are just afraid of being hurt."

I didn't say anything. She was too right.

"So are you going tonight?"

Remember she has a third and final father B'day function this evening...

"I don't know."

We parted on fairly good terms; such as our terms go.

Home, a bit of writing, a phone call or thirty from her. Then/again, phone call, 4:30 PM:

"Are you picking me up?"
"Yes, if you drive."
"OK."

We we're on our way to another family affaire, West Covina style.

I remember Chinese New Years. I remember it with her. I remember it this year; parties: three—count them, three. *Three days of being Chinese.* I was going to write a long poem of a book, titled that. I never quite got around to it.

En route and on the way; me driving, not her, as pre-promised, *"You must get my Uncle something." "Why?" "He's throwing the party. He likes plants. Get him a plant."* So a large, mega heavy clay potted, several brands, of several flowering plants, I got him.

"It's my father's birthday. You should get him something."
"What did you get him?"
"Nothing. This can be from us."
"Thanks!"

An expensive watch on the further exploits of my pushed plastic. But and due to, all-in-all, he's not a bad dude.

We drove, actually I drove, my bad little 356, with the newly arrived spot of red curb paint, thanks to you know whom. We were off, and through traffic, equals we were there.

It was a party, as family parties go. I was the only, *Quai—lo,* (honky), at the scene; no problem. Most in attendance got tilted,

I hung tough—no alcohol if you please. Most of the dudes talked shit, as dudes generally do. I could have joined in but with only a family member(s) to discuss shit with, it did not seem quite appropriate.

"Have you ever had a massage in Bangkok? Don't worry, I won't tell her..." A question asked by an off-going Naval Officer of a cousin. Off, to an Asian post. I did not answer. She, my main and current, L.A. babe, was staring at me.

But, for the record, you must experience it, to understand it. Imagine a glass wall with a hundred or more of the most beautiful women you could desire; pick a number, any number. A schoolboy's dream. Then, a bath, a massage of sorts, and then a *'FUCK,'* as they like to call it. Oh yes, you must experience it! It is the source of poetry...

So, done and gone, introduced to her twenty—two-year-old virgin ballerina, philosophy major babe, of a cousin. She dug my scene. She told her, (you know the one), that she did, *"I don't usually like guys with long hair but he is so cute."*

Obviously, I dug her scene, as well. Where it can/will go, is the only ques—t—ion.

She has what I want!

Lips of the innocent.

The homeboy uncle, who's house it was, tilted to the max; gives me the, *no comprenda english,* "I like you. I love you. I never forget you..." That, and in association with, a full-on hug; as I was to depart.

Home, my place, she was horney. *"Way horney,"* as she so eloquently put it.

Thus, I put IT to her big time. Then, to sleep.

6:00 AM, I am awoken by the sound of the rain upon my patio; a gift from God.

I down a pair of sweatpants and go outside to move my now seriously rusting Italian made easel out of the rain. I fold my drop cloth(s): one plastic, one tarp, and move them and my drying oil painting(s) out of the down pour. The raindrops kissed me like only the embrace of the goddess can do.

Back to sleep, out to breakfast, days go on, as days tend to do.

Time: here I am again. Time, it passes like it is passing now.

So, I guess that is it; up to date, none too late. The babe she is sleeping in my bed; black, the bed, the night, her hair, and the all.

But oh, oh yes, we did make some special love, before she retired to her dreams.

Lights out. Aquarium blue light on. We laid upon Mr. Couch. Soon, our clothing was being removed. A touch, a kiss, a feel in just the right spot—she does it, I do it, we do it so well to—get—her.

Insertion, upon our sides. She, facing me. I, facing her. In and out, back and forth, I lick her breast. Ah fuck, it is perfect.

She moves the vice clamp into place, (her internal vice clamp), a technique of closing in/closing down; she does it just oh so right—like the intoxicating grasp of the perfect wind of love, that one that you never want to be released from.

She grabs the base of my dick with her hand. My dick, inserted deep within her. *"Tighter,"* I say, *"Hold it tight."* She does, and oh, is it heaven. The grasp of her fingers in just the right spot, the vice clamp, shut down tight. Maximum cum, with nothing to lose, could I teach her virgineous cousin this? I don't know. I don't know how anyone could equal the love we make...

...ONE

Awoke to a love, to a sex session on the serious side, to a morning confrontation. The same old story; again...

She was off. Job(s) to seek out in the world; that world, the real world—her world; not mine.

I headed on into L.A. A bicycle frame with a new *groupo* to be picked up and a Belgium Waffle, *Cafe Mocha* session over at FM, (Farmer's Market).

A poem came to me. Came to me while I was there, FM. Came to me as my rushed mind got up to leave and to rush to somewhere else, (somewhere more), with the same no meaning. I didn't write it than in my portable notebook; the one I always carry with me. Didn't write it then, perhaps I will write it now.

*   *   *

I sit here alone
over my shoulder sits a young,
stylish,
and in love couple

glam slam
West Hollywood
fashion passion
in the objective since
I too am you
I too grew from you
you from me

funny how I hate
your implications though

I too have sat there
sat there
in that very same seat
sat there
love
in love
of love
        a babe
        holding onto me

        once or twice
        three babe(s)
        maybe more

put it to the test
love in the words of a poet
claiming immortality
for no reason at all
        the way all poet(s) do

and is it
that we are so different
those of us
who don't quite fit in
        look different
        feel different
        dress different
        act different
different
just the same

is it only we
who hold onto the dream

the dream I have seen fade away
in so many aging eyes
      is it all for nothing
      is it all for something
      nothing from something
      a desire by any other name

yes, I have been in love too
yes, all eyes have gone to me/us
      the girl and I

and when the dreaming is over
and when the truth is spoken
when all the lies
they have come out
      where do we next go
      of what do we next dream
      when no one can see
      who we really are
      what we really are

covered only by the fashion passion
and only by the being different
      let's face it
      no one every really knows
      what is going on inside

love, it sits over my shoulder
love, I have been there before
love, I have longed for it
love, I have run from it
love, what does it mean anyway

I have sat there
sat there in the open
      and yes, I too have been held

held for the night
held for my life
sat there different
different and in love
the perfect place/space to be in
when there is nothing
better to do

*   *   *

A telephone call or several later: pre the poem, during the poem, post the poetry. Tomorrow, I am set up have a three o'clock *rendezvous* to meet—meet on my B'day. She has something planned for me; so came her words.

Day after, Saturday on the calendar of events, no Saturday Jim's—have to hit there come the following day; Sunday.

Saturday speaks of *dunch,* (like brunch, only lunch and dinner, you know), w/ her—her my now main L.A. babe, via Taipei, and her parents: a mother, a father, and a wristwatch. Then, to a party, the same crib as before. This time the younger crowd; *Bon Voyage* to that Naval Officer. Naval Officer with a B'kok massage in mind. (You remember the one).

I have consented with consent never in mind. But you know me: rather reserved, rather introverted, not really wanting to try something new. Well, here I go, so...

And maybe... You never know... A second meet with that desired young virgineous love in mind. You never can tell what may come.

Post the bike, post the FM, post the P.O. Box; a card from Shanghai, (from one of my loves over there). *"Sha Sha."* A card from *me madra.*

Me madra, she gave me $230.00. $200.00 for the sake of $200,00, I guess??? $30.00 implying my thirty-year B'day and all.

Oh boy! So much money! What can I do with $230.00!!! Yeah right...

So anyway, post the several hours of writing which I have done today, the several cup(s) of the java I have drank, the occasional telephone call, and the objective desire to go down and hit the HBHS, (the Huntington Beach Health Spa), a bit later tonight. (You never know what I might find—in the terms of the female department). Here I sit and here I am.

A dream last night of winning on number twenty-eight in Viva Las Vegas. Should I go? I guess not. Five hours on the hard road; not really feelin' it.

The babe, the well-spoken of one, I guess she will be around post the big three— out there on Saturday, w/ an invite to a dinner; Chinese food, no doubt. Out there to a party, Mandarin spoken, also no doubt. And there she will be, in all of her fading and used glory on Sunday morning; four years younger than I, but looking four years older. Well, at least I wasn't the one who abused it.

I look up to a goddess of Tibet. She adorns the space of the wall above me. A goddess *thanka* that I purchased there; Lhasa, Tibet.

I want to return to her bosom. I want to return to her dream; her illusion. I remember the vision of how she showered gold upon me as I made my first airborne accent, over her mountains; airborne decent into her holy valley. I remember. Yes, I remember.

The dreams, they are the same, as they have long been; who knows what they mean. Another day, another night; yeah tomorrow, it is just another day. Tomorrow, my thirtieth B'day.

...night—time ONE

Picked up a few catfish for my A—quar—re—um. An aquarium full of cichlids. Then, moved down south to the HB, Health Spa. A little encounter in the J—CUZ—A and dry sauna with this Chinese/Vietnamese babe of an apparent twenty-year-old who gave me an oh so fine, get out of the water, shot of the sides of her newly shaved beaver. Oh, yes! It was almost like younger days, the pup almost wanted to pop up. But, I am older now and could just feel the circulation in that die—rec—shi—on.

She had four earrings in one of her ears. I comment I had the same. She had two in the other. I commented I have three.

We talked of Vietnam, how I have tried to get in; but no-go as of yet. We spoke of Hong Kong—of how she was a refugee there for a year. We spoke of America and how many, like she and her family, were not as rich as many of those from Vietnam which now swim the swamps of the good ole U.S.A. We spoke of how I would be thirty tomorrow. *"Oh, now you must start thinking of settling down and starting a family,"* she claimed with a longing look of possibility in her eyes.

The perfect present. The perfect gift. A chance in the dance. I love the chance.

As it be told, I basically be booked for this weekend, though... No doubt, I would throw it all away for a night/this night or tomorrow, with her. I chilled though. Played it cool. She is there every night, (so she says);

every night with book in hand. *"Keeps away the creeps,"* she told me.

And me, *"Me, I am here generally Tuesdays and Thursdays."* She wanted to know. She asked. I told her.

Love in the making, romance for the taking. *"Well, it was nice meeting you, see you later,"* I said.

Another time baby. Another time...

So, I will play it this weekend, play it with my main L.A. squeeze. Play it for power, for control, for retribution. The power to keep my eye(s) on my babe. I will exit the control of and for the same; the retribution, she has a gift in mind??? And dinner for a given watch.

All equaling nothing. Nothing all the same. But somewhere in that nothing, I may find a something; a virgin cousin at another cousin's going away party. From which, and because of, I may have material to write about in the future. Gotta live if you want to have something to write about...

A night on the town and afternoon embarking: 3:00 PM; she wants me to be ready tomorrow.

Time will tell as it always seems to do— like the girl I never saw the next day, skating by me, in bicycle riding shades...

Incidentally, I have since purchased the new, more modern pair I spoke of.

Time will tell, as it always seems to do; like the dream of love, I had for her; my new and main L.A. babe, who I now try to exit from. Dreams die hard.

Too far in. Too far out. Saturday night I will ask her for my gift. The gift; to please just leave me alone.

...THIRTY

9:46 AM, a telephone call from my mother, wished me the best.

I think I mention(ed) her proposed *rendezvous* in Viva La Vegi, didn't I??? Yeah, I really want to go there with her... I'm being facetious, of course.

The convo, it was congenial, usually we argue. *No problema.*

Her call awoke me from a dream, a dream I was having where I was arguing with my aunt; her sister. I was yelling at her but instantaneously tuning it off to be polite to this *mulatto* looking, fine thing of a chick, in a secretary-style miniskirt, who entered by dream. Oh yeah! *Once you taste black, you never go back.* So, they say, anyway. Tasted it but never hung around...But, you never know what the future will hold?

l0:15 AM, the now main L.A. ori—ent—al babe gives me the love call on the telephone line(s).

"Are you going to be ready at three?"
"Really! You don't have to do anything for me..."
"Stop being so fucking macho! You know if nobody did anything for you, you'd feel bad."
"Yeah, I guess I'm way ahead of the game. Saturday Jim took me out, my mother sent me $230.00, and you're taking me out..."
"And don't forget my parent's tomorrow. Don't fuck me up again!"

She pauses. She continues…

"This is a lot better than you got last year, a cup cake with a candle in it and you had to pay for the dinner you went out to."

She is referring to my last, main L.A. babe, and my B'day of twenty-nine.

Now she, my last main L.A. babe, is off in Europe somewhere being a stewardess in the skies. A waitress at thirty-five thousand feet. Good riddance…

But actually, I like the idea of a candle in a cup cake…

We; her and I, the previous central and main L.A. babe, we went out to a little Chinese restaurant last year. She continually in the no bucks department; I picked up the tab.

But, anyway back to the central story at hand…

"Are you going to shave?" She inquires.

Me, never being one who particularly like to kept the clean shaven look.

"Maybe…"
"Be ready at three o'clock. Don't being laying around in your baggy house clothes, needing a shave, and your hair looking like an oil pit! Be ready, three o'clock!"
"OK, see you at six."

I was joking…
"Three o'clock!"
"Seven?"

"Stop messing around and remember to bring money and your credit cards."
"What!"
"And, you have to buy me roses for doing all this stuff for you!"

I love selfless giving...

As for today/tonight, I really have no idea what is going on. Time will tell...

Pick up, 3:00 PM and onto whatever dream of inspiration, for the literature, it may hold.

Up...

Kept getting phone calls; couldn't go back to sleep.

I took some morning gin—sing, headed for the shower.

Took a psychic cleansing shower; you know the kind, where you feel your entire being renewed and cleansed. Did the same for the *do*.

Did it as psychically as possible. But, my mind was a bit distracted.

Decided to take myself to a good morning/happy birthday breakfast at this little place overlooking the ocean which I tend to attend; *"One, for the outside please."*

A cup of java or two, a Chinese chicken salad, a more than adorning and lustful glance from this babe of a waitress; done and out~a—there.

As I drove. Well... The actual feeling first came about in the rest—tur—ant of choice. It, the feeling/the thought grew as I drove.

I thought of a *Rolex,* I had seen and she had wanted—she my main and current L.A.

babe. She and I at this high-end jewelry store over in Century City.

I wished I could go, buy it today and give it to her. Though I have purchased her *a Mickey Mouse watch, a Bulova, a Gucci, a Tag Heuer;* still and all, *a Rolex* is the top of the line. But, money it is tight. Yes, tight for sure. Even my plastic is too full for another, run-a-way, romp in the Asian money *never-never land.*

I thought to give her some roses; roses as she desired; $50.00 or $60.00 a dozen. Me, all I could do was play it off, pretend that it is my birthday, not hers. None-the-less, I wish I had the bucks to give her, her the main L.A. babe, which I am trying to bail for, a gift or three. A gift or three, just because...

It kind of brings me down as I type these lines.

I remember a youngster; a yogi. Me, a longtime ago. Shiva Dass, was the name my guru had given me. Sixteen, seventeen, eighteen; my nineteenth birthday, I was studying with him.

I was on the staff of a yoga retreat. The cast and crew asleep: meditation, hatha yoga/karma yoga to practice the next day. We, the leader(s) of the retreat: the Swami(s) and the Yogi(s)—they took me out to a cake and tea session in a restaurant high in the mountains above Santa Barbara when they found out/realized it was my B'day; up there where Pres. Ronnie Regan calls home. Up there where the retreat was being held.

"How old are you?"

"Nineteen."

No one could believe I was so young; so young and a yogi for so long. Look at me now...

To get to the point of the actual story. My guru back then, you know he used to say, on your birthday it is better to give gifts than to receive them. Me too, I have always felt that way.

As I flash back to a time, a long time ago, I realize it was there that I met my than to be—one of my first, (well, maybe second), main and central L.A. babe. Much the same temperament and personality as my current one; even and including a way long dick list. Also, and in addition to, she was a Leo; a Leo, just as is the babe spoken of in this story near complete.

Her/she, that babe way back then; into something I didn't want to be into; loving someone I didn't want to love. Ten years later, here I am, I haven't learned my lesson yet— haven't learned a goddamned thing, I guess. Still playing/living the same melodrama

Hit my P.O. Box...

Simplicity, though I seek it, though I crave it. But in truthfulness; how complex is my life?

L.A. joy(s): check the action at the bad P.O. Box an occasional HBHS, a bike ride or thirty, Thursday at FM. All simplistic...

You look at it that way, yes, I embrace simplicity. Well then, why does it/my life all feel so goddamned complex.

In the box, hoping for a card, birthday present of dreams, whatever... A small wrapped package of a looking thing, a letter, and *dos* post cards; not to mention a bill or three.

The post card(s) from the SF basket case. I told you, I still get them from her...

Funny joke almost, I just wrote the story of her and the card(s), they come...

One told me she would be in L.A. from the 23rd to the 25th, staying at the Biltmore Hotel. Who cares! The other read, *"Hello, I told my dad about you. He told me I should tell you I am not a mental case or sinister or sick. I want your love. You are such a sex bomb. You are alright. I am OK. Love Nanci."*

Oh, as it turns out, I got her name via her letters. Again, who cares!

I open another letter; this one held a uck drawing from her. The package, a twelve-page letter from her, as well. Plus, a note pad, from the SF Hilton. I guess she went and stole one of those bad pups. I guess, I don't know...

In the package this ongoing letter. Page-by-page little notes, notes of saying nothing, to eyes that did not even wish read them. Definition(s) only knowable to a mind lost in the realms of abstract/causal insanity.

The letter, fuck it! I don't have time to read her babbling bullshit. She has sent me those long ones before—also unread.

As I glanced at the sporadic nonsense, I see the word, *"Gurdjieff,"* mentioned. So, I read on; if only for a bit... She saw the movie, *Meetings With Remarkable Men.* So have I, ten years the previous. She associates him,

Gurdjieff, with me; for I gave her a bit of my traditional spiritual rap. But, he is not like I. Not like I, not at all. He had a few good things to say, well-meaning and all, but he, like the movie, did not tell the whole tale. For you see before his Sufi training was completed, he bail-skayed with the book of teachings. Thus, never really understanding them all.

Ah, the western mind, wants it all NOW.

If you don't believe me, read O.M. Burks, *Among The Dervishes.*

So, the letter(s), I will put them where I put all my letters in a shoebox, housed in a cupboard, above my bathroom sink. Her vibes are more polluting than most... My best inclination prefers to just throw them away. My best inclination; but my choice of documentation, a life of documentation, I keep them, anyway. Also kept, just in case, she goes shit-fuck nuts in my direction; someway/somehow...These, the letter(s)/her letter(s) a possession to show her mind.

And vibes, they eventually fade.

Now, I will chill back for a few; a few it can only be. Three o'clock, it is on the horizon; it is approaching and I have to go and do whatever it is she, my main L.A. babe, has planned for us to do.

They say, I have heard it said, people like me become isolated in their intellect, in their own mind. So, and thus, I choose the seeking of unknown answers in the realms of unknown question in the occult; seeking unknown answers, in the arms and in/of the distraction(s)/illusion(s) of illicit women. Wouldn't want to be become isolated, would I?

My main L.A. babe tells me I seek salvation for my earthly deeds/sins in the arms of mysticism. Maybe...

For all any of that is worth... Well, it general; all equals nothing.

Descriptions, answers, and a fool's cries in the night. I am getting older. The world is getting colder. And, if nothing else, this text has given me the perception that I must write more prolifically. I need to work on one book, (more directly), at a time. And, do it everyday. Instead of the opposite—having over twenty books in various stages of completion and many more in/on my mind.

I believe I will have to write a 30+1 description and decoding of the day(s) that are to come.

Seeking my own solitude, I have become lost in loneliness. Lost in my own intellect, I have set myself apart. The day, today, the party dinner, and the party tomorrow; attempt(s) at coming out.

But parties, I don't really like 'em. And people who need to have people around them all the time are nothing when they are alone.

Life is a paradox.

Thirty, I don't know what to do. But I don't feel too bad; kinda good, kinda positive.

The day looks good. I look outside. I see the ocean. I see the sun. No place I'd rather be.

Well, that is a debatable issue...

...THIRTY + ONE

In a lim—oh—sine...
You know, like that Rick James song.
I guess it is a few years old now... But,
it is still played, on the RA—DEE—Oh.
Classic of an era in the making....

To tell the story...
A call from the intercom,
"Your limosine is waiting."

I didn't blink...
"I will be down in a few minutes."

Always keep 'em waiting...
So, I was dressed as per request, *"You
must be ready at three o'clock!"* Remember...
Actually, it was more like 2:40, but no
real problem. I had just cleaned the apartment
a bit, put my clothing on, and was sitting
back/laying back on Mr. Couch awaiting the
arrival of what I did not know was to come.
As it turns out, the arrival was a limo.
Down; the dude waiting at the door of
my building; escorts me to the car. The
limousine, *Ultra-Stretch,* I prefer the
Presidential-Stretch, (the larger/longer ones,
for the uninitiated)... I mean hey, if you're
going to rent a penis extension, you may as well
go all the way! But, and in any case...
It was a few years old; the limo that is...
The model and make, a bit used inside;
obviously it was an econo—rental. Not my

style. But then, I didn't rent it and I wasn't going to pay for said.

The babe she always complains about her lack of the bucks, so she obviously shopped the marketplace; seeking the best deal and all...

But then, on the other side of the picture and/or coin, no other babe has ever rented me a limo.

The driver, he was a dude, obviously straight off the boat from Israel. Personally, I always go for the blonde female drivers. It makes for a better arrival on the scene. But, that is just me... The dude/the driver, personable enough. New to the game, obviously. Had to ask me how to get to the freeway. I told him and I also told him I had to make a stop at the local florist on the way.

Yes, en route, I did buy her a dozen of the red and long stemmed, $65.00, if you please—roses in a gold box. Rose(s) in hand, we were off.

The exact location of our arrival was not known to me. Maybe two days back we had passed this Sunset B.L.V.D., West Hollywood hotel haven of the rich and famous. She made a comment about it, so I thought, *'Maybe?'*

As we drove down the mid-afternoon freeway, I clicked on the L.A. classical station of my pre—fer—ants, and chilled back in the freedom of Haydn and the lost feelings of time lost—time lost, long ago.

I could not help but remember, (the thoughts they came to mind), of that ride I took with my previous, main, and thankfully long-gone, L.A. babe; of, (as mentioned), now a stewardess/waitress in the friendly skies. She had an art piece in an art show. The L.A. mayor, Tom Bradley, presided over the opening. I went and picked her up—she then worked at a museum; L.A. County Museum of Art. She sold people their ticket(s) in; at the ticket window. But, that day, back then, there she was in front of the museum; waiting for me—surprised with a limo to the/her opening.

I picked her up right after her shift. She stood in front, on Wilshire B.L.V.D. Dressed in black; her long Spanish locks braded and pulled tightly back, into a ponytail—pure elegance, pure style.

That was a different time though. That was a different limo service. It, the limo, was new and presidential; perfect inside, unlike this ride—mine; the one I now rode in. It definitely was not this/the econo version; though the radio station I listened to was the same.

110, Pasadena Freeway, North; the downtown exit; we were getting off. The *Bonaventure Hotel,* we, (her and I), had stayed at and had a special time or three there before.

Yes, she was a romantic; she, my now main, L.A., via Taipei, babe; who I just basically wanted to leave. Yes, she was, like I, a romantic.

Up in front we pull up. The driver, he walks around to let me out. He needed a signature; I offered mine, on her credit card bill.

As I write these words, the thought does come to mind, knowing her, (understanding her), she may not pay said bill—dispute it; claim she didn't sign it. She always looks for ways out. She stopped payment on a check or three of money that she has owed to me—did this, more than a time or two. So, I can just see the limo company coming after me for payment...

Awh, life... With babe(s) I never really wanted to be with, and all the problems there of and therefore. It just all isn't worth it... Or, is it?

But, I will cross that bridge when and if it comes. The bridge of an unpaid limo bill and all...

So, I am out, in the door, to the desk; they wouldn't give me the room number. They have this bullshit little policy; no room number give out(s)...

I suppose that I understand, but NOW it has fucked me over. So me, I go and call the room. She was not in. I ask the op—er— ator. *"We can't tell you what room it is..."* This, even though, I am suppose to crib there.

I was about to get pissed, get a taxi, and leave, when I feel a grab from behind. It was her. She; it was she.

She hadn't told them the room was for two. As the story goes... $15.00 less if it is only for one. How fucking stupid! All this for $15.00.

She had gone to meet the limo, meet the limo, and buy me a rose; *uno.* I handed her a dozen.

"Why did you do that? It spoils my surprise of the one I have gotten for you?"
"You said that for all you are doing, I had to buy you roses."
"Did I say that?"

She always forgets what she says. Most of the time she says things she doesn't even realize that she has said—but that's a different story, of course.

Up in the room, twenty—seventh floor; view of the hills, the Hollywood Hills, and of the city down below.

The view was nice. I like to look down at the city and the smog of the fading Summer. We were two days past the first day of Autumn.

We lay in bed for a little bit of a love embrace, the full-wall mirror behind the bed reflecting the essence of the love mode. A gift in action, a gift of passion, *loved lived too long,* I did her. But, I felt nothing.

Out, seemed to be the call. A walk around the hotel; a momentary discussion of how I liked living in hotels—it is all so fucking simple; the place is clean(ed), the dirty clothing just sent OUT—life, it is easy and creativity it is so close at hand.

We walked the floors of retail, tried to find a Bonaventure tee-shirt. But, none in existence. We passed the massage parlor, third floor.

"Do you want one?"
"No."

But, she tried to set me up anyway. An aging Japanese/American lady: nimble and willing fingers at hand,

"I can do you now."
"No thanx."

"Oh, he's just shy..."

I wanted to say, *"Believe me, I am anything but shy."* With B'kok, more time than I can count, under my belt; believe me, I am not shy.

Actually, I just wanted to save my main and central babe's dwindling *danero*. Too nice of a guy, I know...

She, my main L.A. and vanishing babe, being the junk food junkie that she is, decided on a little frozen yogurt. I paid.

Outside we sat. After a few moments, she jumped up, *"I'll be right back,"* she said and was out of there.

I sat there: outside, downtown L.A., looking inside the windows at all the restaurants which adorned the hotel walls; inhabited with no customers. I wondered how they stayed in business. I looked around; saw the massive man-made structures surrounding me. The air cool. The night coming on. This place, it was definitely placed upon my list of L.A. bohemia.

I spooned at the melting frozen yogurt, trying to be a gentleman and save her some as I waited. But, the waiting got a little weird, a little long. Fifteen minute later; return. She came, birthday cake box in hand.

In all her, *not give a fuck style,* she ripped it open. Thirty—one candles had been placed upon the top. One to grow on and all...

Lighting all thirty-one of them was not easy, however. The wind, it gently blew. She used a lighter; a lighter from another time, a time maybe two months the previous, when I had run off to Asia and she, disenchanted with life, had begun her ritual of smoking cigarettes again.

She lighted them. The wind blew them out. Finally, two were going. AOK. That's good enough for me.

I wished for...

Well, I can't tell you that... But, I blew them out.

A wish in the making, a dream for the taking.

The cake: carrot. The yogurt: vanilla and coconut. I got sick.

She wanted a java. I found the place. They had *cappuccino,* as well. She still preferred a java. She had a java, I had a *cappuccino;* at my expense.

She wanted to walk out onto the city; follow the footbridges over the streets of downtown—follow them to the other man-made structure(s), follow them to wherever they may lead.

The cake got put in the room. The walk got put into motion.

We walked... We sat by a nuevo—Japanese pond of a watertight structure. Felt the day, in the wind, close down. We walked underground to a nuevo—below the surface shopping mall; way scary. We took a nuevo—Escalator in motion to the surface; held in limbo by this secretary version of a mega big butt black chick doing the way slow Negro walk; trying to impress somebody. Who, I do not know? Her, attempting to exerciser her power(s) of control over somebody, keeping us from our appointed no—destination(s), by ineffectively creeping her high heels along as slow as possible. Finally, outside...

"What's that?"
"The Biltmore."
"Lets go. I've never seen it."
"Oh, it's nothing. Just another hotel."
"Have you been there?"
"Yeah, maybe ten years ago. I saw a spiritual lecture there."

Actually, it was Daya Mata from the SRF.

"It's nothing special!"

Remember, the SF psycho bitch in her last letter was supposed to be there: 23rd to the 25th... Did not want to get into that!

"Oh, you're so boring. You're no fun."

You see, she always likes to throw in comments like the above in order to get her own way. Needless to say, we went...

Basically, I prayed we did not see the previously described, said, SF psycho bitch.

Inside, the palace-like structure; fifty foot ceilings, chandlers; we behaved like little children. We took a picture or three, well maybe four.

You see, to tell the back-story, she had this little thirty-five-millimeter camera in tow, which I had purchased at Disneyland, the time we had gone, maybe five months ago. $110.00 at the *Disneyland Camera Shop* on Main Street.

She had to have pictures that day. It, the camera, had actually accompanied me on my last journey to Asia as I like to take a small and portable camera along, to complement my more than massive other camera collection, that I take with me wherever I go.

Back in the sack, however, upon my return, I chalked that up to one of the numerous gifts which she, from me, has received.

We jumped around the hotel; went place(s) which we were not supposed to go. So on and so forth...

It was an obvious relief to leave, however, unsighted, (by you know who). We agreed, it would be a way cool place to stay, next time, downtown, around.

We walked back as the nighttime colors were coming on. The camera again served its purpose. Construction, art works, the rise and demise of modern mankind; it all made a more than beautiful backdrop for some exchanged photographs.

Back in the room, still some time to kill before our eight o'clock dinner engagement at the restaurant on the top floor, we lay in/on the bed.

She was tired, having not slept much the night before. Her roomy, (you remember the one who just had a B'day party that I didn't attend), dumped by her boyfriend. *"Happy Birthday!"*

"Catatonic," is how she, my main L.A. babe, described her. As such and because of, she gave her, her bed as generally her roomy sleeps on the couch.

After hearing the story, I grabbed her a card/sent her a card, *"Feel better! You deserve to be happy."* Sent it from the hotel.

So her/she, my main and current L.A. babe, not used to the lack of her, *oh so precious all-cotton sheets and down comforter,* well, so I am told, she got little or no sleep upon the couch evening last.

We lay in bed, but we did not sleep.

Later: upstairs in the restaurant, a nice booth. AOK. I ordered a bottle of wine from a so-so, at best, wine list. I drank a glass, didn't like it. I drank no more.

Dinner: lobster and filet minion; not bad.

The check came, *"Are you going to sign,"* I ask. *"Sign for $122.00."* She replies. Sign only to spend the rest of my life hearing her complaints about it. I pay...

Then, she gets into the old and boring conversation of, *"When am I going to give her some money? She needs money! When will I give her that money?" Why haven't I given her mega money before?"* To keep the peace, I say, *"Tomorrow. I'll give you some money tomorrow."*

On the way back to the room, she hits the hotel head. En route, she sees someone she knows.

The fact of the matter is, it is virtually fucking impossible to ever go anywhere without seeing someone she knows. It is real bullshit and I hate it!

You know what I am saying? She is one of those exceedingly outgoing people and all...

Fuck that again! Quality, not quantity, that is what I believe life is all about.

This case... It was some dude from Art Center, (where, as previously stated, she had gone to school). This case... It was some dude, apparently one of her classmates, way back when. Now, he worked at this hotel. Shows you where all that money spent at going to *Art Center* will get you.

He/this one was one of those typical West H'wood tourists looking mutha' fuckers with the bullshit, now hip to wear, (you must wear one), ponytail, and all that...

No real words were spoken. Just glances at a distance, from across a room.

I asked her/stated/said, *"Did she stare at him; stare like her grandmother did at me that night at her father's, buy him a watch, birthday party?"* It was a deadly stare.

For the record, she, the old, grandmother, sat there the whole night; eyes on me, dead stare. I just didn't pay attention, but it was haunting—her eyes never leaving me. But then/now I know where her, my main L.A. babe, got the invocation and the training to dead stare at people the way she does. I don't like it!

Back in the room, it was not the all night, take a bath with candles, make love three-hundred times, in three million positions, that we had enjoyed the last time around at this hotel. She was tired; *no problema.* A candle was lighted; one. A soda was drank; two—one each. The radio was tuned to this old blues station that I like down in LB, (Long Beach). Reason being, she doesn't dig opera and that be

what be blaring on the classical music side of
the radio dial.

We made love, slowly passionately;
once. She went to sleep. I lay there reflecting
about life: the why(s), the feeling(s), the how
did I get in this mess(es) with her, and the how
could I get out. Mostly, I visualized better
times, better ways.

Today, I was thirty years old.
Just another day...

*   *   *

night time scream(s)
and it whisper(s)
speaking to god
show me a better way

night time scream(s)
in its silent violence
are we really
so all alone

and when you lay there
quite as you can be
you can almost feel
the mysticism
it becomes so real

I scream
in the night time
when the world is so asleep
I scream
for understanding
god tells me

to quit being such a whimp

nigh time sound(s)
of the city below
singing to my ears
    in too deep
    out too deep
    yes, I hear
    but what
    does it say to me

I lay in the bed
king size
with a girl
who I have tried to love
and, for a moment
believed that it was so

I lay in bed
king size
I try
I try so hard
but there is just nothing there
nothing left
nothing
left for me to love

night time scream(s)
in its existence
how did I get in so deep
night time scream(s)
in its knowledge

I listen
but I hear nothing

*   *   *

Sleepless nights, in thought(s) of passion; I have not been sleeping so well of late.

She did her usual go to the bathroom three or four times, throughout the encounter of the evening. Then, the morning came.

A nothing shower, in each other's arms. I watched her as she steals the bathroom rug; a towel or two or three. Said she wanted to get her money's worth. But stealing is stealing as far as I'm concerned... And, it is not good.

I remember back to our first date, I invited her to go to SF. Yes, L.A. to SF on our first date—after only one telephone call. Sounded like a good idea at the time... It was not.

San Fran—cis—co Hilton Penthouse Suite; $500.00 at night. She wanted to steal the sheets. Then, she told me I was stuffy, when I would not let her do so. She wanted to go swimming. She hadn't brought a bathing suite. She wanted to go naked. Told me I was a prude when I suggested it was not a good idea.

I remember the drive back and down South, down to L.A. I kept questioning, *'How did I let myself get so involved with a woman of no mind, no time, no class, so rude. Why didn't I just walk away? Put her on an airplane.'*

Funny story... Short, made long.

SF drive to L.A. It was misery. She smoked and smoked and smoked—bitched and bitched and bitched. I got her back to her West

H'wood crib. You know the one just up the street from, *The Whiskey*. Got her there; parked. Helped her get her stuff upstairs. Being a gentleman and all… Got her up there; was about to leave. But, someone in her building was having a party. Several cars had instantaneously parked in her driveway, behind me. No way out! It was like god was playing a bad joke on me. No way out! So, here we are today.

That was like ten months ago…

So, we checked out of the hotel. I jumped up as the elevator went down. Have you ever tried that? The feeling is really fun.

There was a family; a black dude and his two sons. He probably told them don't end up like that guy: thousand-dollar Italian birthday suite on and jumping up in a downward traveling elevator.

In fact, as memory serves, I had done it earlier the day before; an elevator full of tourists: aging and old, looking at the city through the walls of the glass elevator that skims the side(s) of the *Bonventura Hotel*. Freedom, I sought the freedom.

It has not always been that way. Ten months the previous, ten months before; me, right out of an uptight/alright relationship with an, oh so fine elegant model of the dreams; so proper, she was so well groomed. No one had ever taught me how to jump up in the downward moving elevator(s), or the reason why. SF, San Fran—cis—co; ten months, a lifetime ago. Her, the one I was with then; ten months ago, and now, she has become the main L.A. babe. It was she who had taught me how.

Others were in the elevator, there/then; back then—ten months ago. I asked her to chill down, as it made all those uptight SF people, way tense. But, that was then, she had a point to prove, I guess; rebellion against class and money—someone else's class and money.

So, where has it all gone? Now, I am so much more free—free and anti-sophisticated. I jumped. She didn't. I guess I owe her something; a ticket back to the freedom of a different time.

She has gotten old in these ten months. I have grown younger.

The Express Check Out in the slot; down into the gay—raj. To her car, not the limo.

They, the valets, had trouble finding it; twenty minutes later, three complaints later, they, the valets, drive it up. We are out.

Breakfast at a little lo—cal dinner, put it on my tab. I make the comment, *Rolex,* Century City. We are on our way.

Now, there I was lost in the dilemma. What do I do? How do I play it? I want to give her something, I want to give her everything; psychological payback for the only girl who ever did anything financial for me on my B'day. I mean she did limo me to a hotel.

And, give on my B'day. Well, the day after. You remember that story?

It was tearing me up inside: the yes, the no. What should I do? I could have found a way out. But, what do I do? I did it. I purchased it for her, $1,798.00, the aforementioned, *Rolex.*

There have been others; others I have not given the deserved amount to. There have been those; those I have given way too much undeservingly to; i.e, this girl in China; the P.R.C. I remember, diamond ring(s), I bought her; diamond bracelet(s). I gave to her. It took me more than a year to fully realize all of her words were nothing more than lies. Those like that chick in B'kok: rubies, diamonds, twenty—four carat gold to adorn her golden wrist; a year later all she said (too) had turned into the worst kind of lies.

A fool and his money, they soon go separate ways.

We had a party to be at. Her, my main L.A. babe and I. A going away, naval cousin party. Remember?

I had to change my clothes. So, down to the South Bay; my crib. Clothing changed, present to buy, we go to a shopping mall, and her watch it does not/it stopped working. WHAT!!!

I call the jewelers, scream in pure poetic, irate form. She wanted to go to the party. I wanted to go to the jewelers. *"Let's handle it now; OK!"*

A quick trip back home. Had to get the receipt/the box. A quick drive there. I at the wheel; screaming. I was ready! *"God, I've never seen you like this before, you are so dynamic." "Hey, you just don't mess with Rolex."*

As we studied the form and the conveyance, a drama in a distant night. The watch it had been sold before; warranty signed. What! This is a return! This is fucking no-go in the mega bucks watch world!

It is sometimes funny, as mentioned previously in this text, how things they just seem to fall into place: into form, into time...

We had planned to get the watch engraved. Me, I wanted all future dudes to know it was my gift to her, in the giving. The shop, my main engraving central, *Ma and Pa Kettle,* at the helm; closed on Saturday. Good thing though... Or, I would have had to return an engraved *Rolex.*

She waited in the car. Didn't want to get in the middle. In the car. In the parking lot. It was her hard top jeep, made by *Suzuki,* type thing. I went in to kick ass.

"What are you doing now, selling used Rolexes!"

I said it as I threw it on the glass case. In other words, let's set the tone and the motion, DON'T FUCK WITH ME!

"This is my birthday, and I always like to give someone a gift on my birthday!"

"Oh, that's nice," I'm interrupted.
"No, it is just something that I do." I continue.
"I have a function to be at and this is making me very late. What kind of way is this to business anyway! I have never had this problem with a Rolex dealership before!"
"No excuses, this should never have happened..."

A long story made short, the Armenian babe who sold us the piece—actually, she got my juices flowing, and the honky, wonder white bread chick, they set me up with another time piece. Up'ed the dollar value, changed the face, (silver to back), my babes desire; no charge. Plus, kick back the price fifteen percent.

Apology accepted!

Watch on her wrist. Off to the party; West Covina—a party I didn't want to go to. But, being the nice guy that I am; I went...

En route, traffic jam up and around Coliseum/Sports Arena. A concert going on. We take a drive through Watts to get to another freeway; in place, space, and time.

We had an argument. Well, we always seem to do just that. But, you would think that if someone just gave you a mutha' fucking *Rolex*, you would/could be cool. But, we argued *none-the-less*.

Argument of who I was, who she was, and of how I just found out that en route to the party we had to go all the way to her parent's house, in the Anaheim Hills, to pickup her brother; as he lived there with them.

So, to her parent's house we go. A brother we picked up and chauffeur to the party. A dinner I would have preferred to just say, *"Fuck it,"* to. But, I did not.

Potluck Chinese food was the menu. Again, I was the only *'Qui Lo'*, in tow. Me, I had brought two bottles of the imported vino; (the good stuff), from my personal stash as my/our offering. She, my babe, bought an ugly shirt, for the previously discussed out-going cousin.

The good news, she, the babe, the female babe; twenty—two-year-old virgin ballerina, philosophy major babe, of a cousin, was there. But, she had gotten her *do* permed; uck!

But, the dream(s) of what could be; they still lingered. Virgins and thoughts and all the possibilities. Dream on big guy, dream on...

"You know, she is enamored with you." So she, my main and current L.A. babe, told me.

The younger virgineous cousin, who came and sat by me. Stylish clothes, face of Taiwanese beauty, live it/love it. She is not like the other(s), not a good girl in the making, more like love/available, for the taking. And, no doubt some lucky young buck of the O.C. (Orange County); some *Surf Rat* will probable get to pop that cherry. If I had her number, if I had a choice; believe me it would be a different way.

Post the party, post some Chinese cuisine, post the promise, with my chick's disapproval, to meet her cousin in B'kok, post having my form warmed by the eyes of this (other) serious *cha-cha* babe, (some friend of a friend), we were out-a-there. I was at the wheel of her ride.

There, however, at the party, post the first exhibiting of the new *Rolex,* I was told the story of the day, the mother of the babe, my main and current one, examining the new *Rolex* I had just bought her daughter. She told me, as the story goes, as it was told to me, that Hong Kong 1963; en route Taipei to Sao Paulo; where they, (her family), initially lived in the

Americas. She, the mom, bought he, the dad, a *Rolex;* $300.00 NEW back than. (A lot of money then, not now. The price has gone way up). Three hundred dollars when she only had one-thousand to her name. She bought him a *Rolex* for he wanted a *Rolex.* But, he gave the watch away.

As the family tree goes, so I am told, he always gives everything away. *'Fuck,'* I thought. *'Didn't I just buy him a watch the other day for his B'day? I guess I know where that's going to end up. Glad I spent the money...'*

The story, reiterated to me as we drove by my main L.A. babe, who doesn't like that quality in him either. Fuck me...

In any case, post the party, it was set that we were to meet the family, just an immediate family function, at this sushi stop. Meet we did.

I impressed them with my Japanese linguistic capabilities. My Mandarin sucks...

At the sushi dinner table, the story had to be told once again; the story of giving away the *Rolex.*

Three and counting. This time, the story told, for the ears of the bro's babe who had arrived on scene.

He too, the brother wanted a *Rolex.* A *Rolex* with a steel band, not so different than the model I now wear. I showed it to him. I showed it to them. Her parents grabbed at it; wanted to see it too. *Explorer II model.*

"It keeps time in two time zones."
"Where do you have the other time zone set for?"

"Bangkok."

She, my main and current L.A. babe, grabs it and begins to change the second time zone around.

That's OK, I know the time difference in B'kok. I always know the time in Bangkok...

Then, the discussion goes on; once again, I have heard it all before: to the expensive watches, the expensive jewelry, she my main L.A. babe had gotten from her mother, in her young(er) adolescent. Jewelry she had found. Jewelry she had lost.

Later that evening, I suggested to her that she do something to replace what she had been unconscious with.

"Why? She can't wear it anyway. Now she has allergies!" So rudely I was told.
"That's not the point; consciousness is."

Needless to say, she got pissed. She never likes to hear what she never wants to hear. A bit of an argument ensued; par for the course as the course seems to go.

She is no better than the father she criticizes for giving things away. In fact, worse.

So-so sushi. Very so-so night. Invited to a birthday function for the bro, one week in the future. Think I will pass...

In bed and to sleep, she continued to snore in my ear. In bed and to sleep; awoken by the snoring; kept that way by her *silent but deadly* Chinese food/Japanese food nighttime farts; uck!

Morning woke; I told her the story of my lack of sleep, due to said. She laughed; said nothing embarrasses her. She has no shame. I guess that is her/our problem.

...EPILOGUE

Saturday Jim's on Sunday, traveling cup of ice java in my hand. Should I now state, 30+1+2+3+4? For Tuesday, here I sit...

Sunday, S.J. and I, we helped Mopi, his neighbor, pull tree stumps from his yard.

I gave my godchild, S.J.'s daughter, a set of walkie-talkies, which she had desired. Another birthday gift, given to another; not her's but mine—a day later/a day after.

He, S.J., told me how cool I had been initially not showing up for her, my main and central L.A. babe's, two birthday parties; the night he, his family, and I, went out to my B'day dinner. Remember? He told me how cool I had been no-showin' for her dad's hundred dollar a plate, Monterey Park, birthday dinner. He told me I was cool but now I was a fool, putting a *Rolex* on the girl's wrist. Guess he was right... Mega bucks on the arm of a babe I never even really wanted to be with—mega bucks I don't have.

P.O. Box on the way home, *dos cards, dos mas,* cards from the SF nut job. You know the one I oh so luckily avoided at *The Biltmore.* She stated some nonsense about something and said that she saw me at MY concert/that traffic jam of a concert at the Coliseum/Sports Arena the day before.

Then, I began to realize what her twisted mind was thinking... She had mentioned something to the effect in one of her previous letters which I had never really read but only glanced at...

180

You see, there is this rock star/movie star that people continually compare my looks to his. I mean, I don't see it; not when you look close and he is five or six years older than me. So, is it a complement or insult? I never know which.

But, the basket case obviously thinks I am that guy—twisted mind/twisted time; actually, I feel a bit sorry for her.

Life and its passions, life and its pain, some just take the toll harder than others.

Another letter in the P.O. Box from my newest B'kok babe. But, that is a story waiting to happen...

Home, I try to think of a way to get two G's together, to pay off all the bills on my Platinum AMEX. My life...

So, that is basically the story—as all stories must come to an end... This is the end of this one.

I am now a few days over thirty years of age.

As for my now and main L.A. babe, I am, as usually, trying to bail.

Obviously, I love her. She is just a fucking stunning, *glam slam,* pure style, Taiwan via West H'wood, beauty. And, she fucks like there is no tomorrow. Obviously, I hate her. We are so different; so at odds.

She comes out ahead, however, *Rolex* and all.

But, the fact of the matter is, without her, and all this life confusion, this would not have been much of a story to tell; the story, *Ten to Thirty.* And, due to and the *none-the-less,* because of, she helped to make it, this story/my life what it is.

Life and time, it has all been so seemingly full, in the recent days.

So... See you the next time around...

*   *   *

winds of change
winds of pain
let the rain fall down on me
     give me a reason
     any one will do
     give me a purpose
     give me a lie
     I hear them all the time
night time(s)
day time(s)
living in the wind
     reason to come
     reason to die
     worth nothing
     worth something
     I don't know
     I just don't know
     so I pretend

S.
88.27.9
Redondo Beach, California